AIN'T NO SUNSHINE

KATHERINE JAY

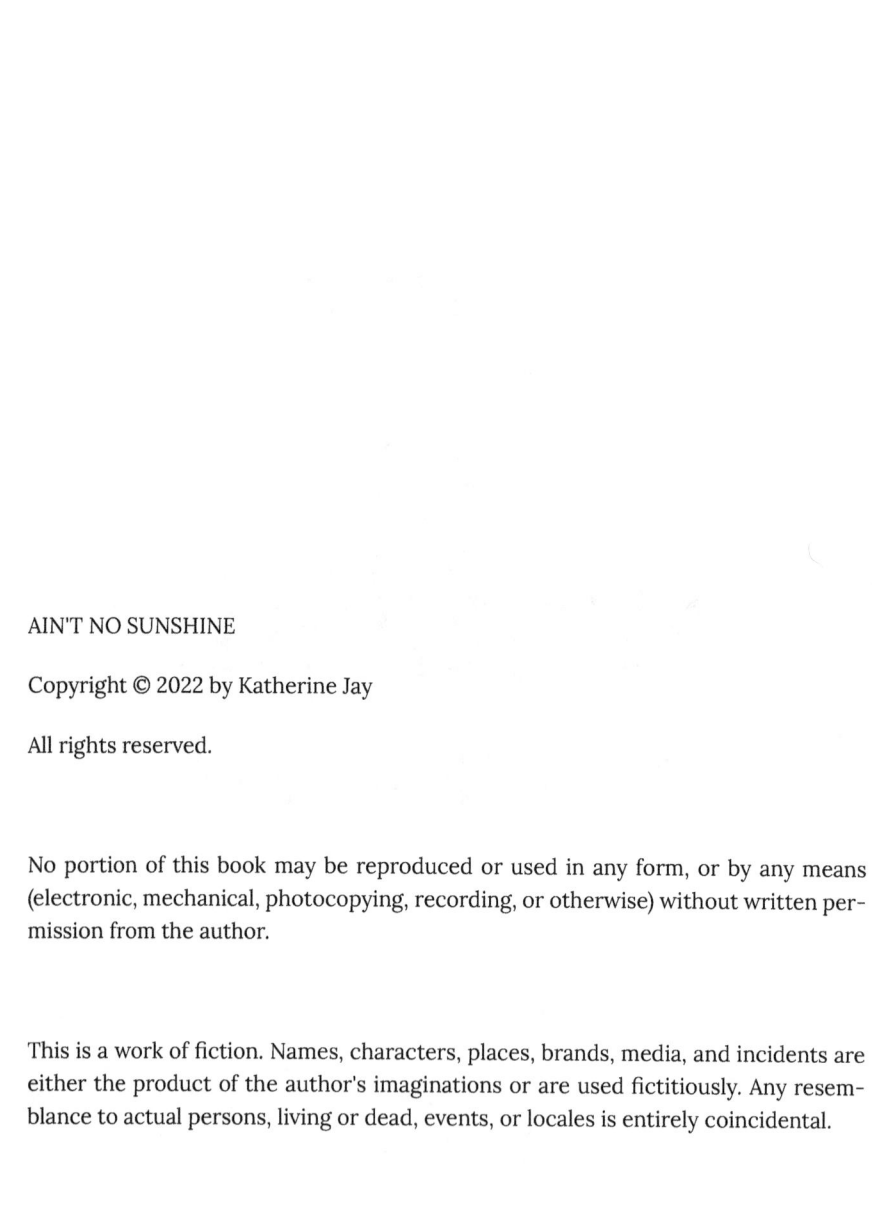

Contents

To everyone who believed I could do this, even when I didn't.
You rock!

Chapter One

Cory

My head slips from the hand it's resting on, snapping me from yet another daze. *Ugh! What was the professor saying?* I blink a few times, just as chairs scrape along the floor; papers rustle and people rise in their seats around me, confirming I've missed most of the class. A class normally meant for juniors and I'm a freshman. *Shit!* And, I'm pretty sure today was important. *Every day is important, Cory.*

I need to get it together. Fast. Before, one, I fail this class, or two, he catches me staring. Nate Edwards. The guy I can't seem to get out of my head. We've shared a class all semester, and it's safe to say I've struggled to focus. I don't know what it is about him, but from the moment I saw him, I haven't been able to get him off my mind. It could be his tall, lean body, his boyish good looks, or the way he throws his head back when he laughs. It could be the warm smiles he doles out or the dimple he gets when he seems genuinely happy. Really, it could be all of those things, or none. But something has me drawn to him.

My best friend, Summer, tells me I'm crazy. She doesn't understand why I wouldn't just ask him out. *Like it's that easy.* She's extremely confident when it comes to men. Actually, even that's putting it mildly. She takes what she wants, when she wants it. I'd be jealous of her confidence if it didn't scare the hell out of me. I'm more of a wait-for-him-to-notice-me kind of gal, and despite that not doing me any favors, I have no plans to change.

I sneak another glance Nate's way before standing and following the crowd like a sheep. I'm shoving my notebook into my bag, lost in thought, when I accidentally bump into the person in front of me and stumble backwards. Strong arms grip me from behind as the person ahead of me spins around.

"Sorry, I wasn't watching where I was going," I apologize as heat rises up my chest.

"No sweat; I barely noticed it. You're too small to even move me," he responds, and I recognize him as one of the football players. I should be grateful for my small structure, but his mention of it makes me redden even more.

I smile and try to shake off my embarrassment just as a warmth spreads over me, and I suddenly realize that the hands that caught me are still gently holding my waist. "Are you okay?" a deep voice whispers into my ear. A voice that I would know anywhere. Nate.

Of all the people in this massive class...

I try to school my features and turn to look over my shoulder, but he's a lot closer than I thought, and my nose almost brushes his cheek. Quickly, I inhale and then feel myself flushing red again. "Thank you for catching me. I'm good now."

"You sure?" he says with a devastating smile as his stunning hazel eyes lock with mine. The tips of his fingers brush the skin under my top and I have to work hard to stop myself from reacting to the fire it lights inside me. I realize I still haven't answered, as his hands grip me tighter for a second before letting go, leaving me instantly missing his touch, but snapping me out of my daze.

"Positive. Thank you," I say, grateful that I'm finally able to use my words.

"Anytime." He winks and then moves past me to exit the room. I brush a loose hair behind my ear as I try to control my erratic heartbeat and bite my lip to stop a giddy smile from forming. *Because did that really just happen?* Slowly, I shake my head at the shock, and when I look up to walk out the door, I find Nate's pained gaze staring back at me. My breath catches, and I can't help but wonder if maybe I could have caused that look, until he notices me staring and smiles, causing me to redden all over again. *He doesn't even know you, Cory.*

He sends me another wink before walking away to meet his friends, and, embarrassment aside, I can't stop the smile that graces my face.

When I arrive home, Summer's studying in her room. It's our last week of classes before finals begin. Hence the reason I should have been paying attention. I walk in and flop back onto her bed with a sigh. "Oh, Summer, life is good."

She looks up at me with laughing green eyes and shakes her head, accustomed to my optimistic love of life.

We've been best friends since middle school and have lived together since we were sixteen. It's safe to say we know each other almost better than we know ourselves.

She looks back down at her books and I roll my eyes. She's not even going to ask me why I'm so happy. *Typical.* I huff out a laugh and shake my head.

"I'm having a moment here. Pay attention," I say, picking up a pillow and hitting her over the head with it.

She pauses and smirks at me with a raised eyebrow as she laughs. "My apologies. Why is life so good?"

"Nate."

Summer's head flings back with laughter. And yep, I know where this is going. "It's always Nate," she says. "Did something *actually* happen, or was he just *particularly gorgeous* today?" She tries to mock my voice when she says "particularly gorgeous" and she's almost spot on.

"Both." I bite my lip and bounce my eyebrows for extra effect as I sit up.

Summer drops her pen and her face lights up with a warm smile. She's very cynical when it comes to love, but she's always one hundred percent invested in my love life, *or lack of.* "Tell me everything," she says excitedly, and I do. Every. Minute. Detail.

When I've finished my play-by-play of what I'm calling 'the moment', I flop back on the bed, looking over in time to see Summer's eyes widen and a smirk appear on her face. Inwardly, I cringe because I know she's about to suggest something outside my comfort zone. "It's time to talk to him, maybe even ask him out." *Told you.*

I shake my head before she's even finished speaking. "Summer, I—"

"Wait," she says, raising her hand in front of me. "How about this? We're about to go on summer break." *Okay.* "Let's make a deal."

"Ah... what kind of deal?" I say as butterflies swarm my belly just thinking about what she might say.

"If you see Nate *anytime* over the break, you'll ask him out."

"Umm..."

Summer slides over and lays down beside me, linking our hands. "When was the last time you saw Nate during *any* of our breaks?"

I sigh, because she's got me there. I *never* see him. I don't even know if he's from around here or another state. Maybe he goes home? "Never. Not once."

"Exactly." She smiles. "So, deal?"

"Deal," I say and then cover my face in my hands. *What are the chances I'll see him this time?*

Chapter Two

Cory

S *he set me up.* Summer totally set me up. Or, at the very least, made plans to increase the chances of running into Nate *organically*. Ugh! I could just...nothing. I would never do anything. But damn her.

It's been a month since we made that deal, and I'd actually forgotten about it, *almost*. At least, I was no longer thinking about it hourly. I'm currently standing in line to get tickets to some movie I don't even want to see, and guess who's standing ahead of me?

Yep; Nate. Which means I now have a deal to fulfil, and dammit, that terrifies me.

I collect our tickets and turn to meet Summer where she's waiting at the entrance, immediately scowling when I see the hint of a smirk she's trying to hide. She raises an eyebrow. "What's that look for?"

"You know exactly what it's for," I mumble with a pout.

She laughs, curling one of her long blonde locks around her finger. "You're right; I do. But it was a complete coincidence. Sort of. Mostly."

"I'm listening," I say expectantly, running my hand through my copper brown hair and probably messing it up. God, I hope Nate's not seeing the same movie.

Summer crinkles her nose. Something she does often when she's a little uncomfortable. "I *may* have overheard a guy from the football team say he was meeting Nate here. On this day. At this time."

I shake my head, but before I can speak, Summer cuts me off. "Look, it *was* a complete coincidence that I heard that conversation. I was filling up my car, and he *happened* to be filling up at the pump next to me while chatting with some girl through the window."

And, of course, her story sounds legit. *At least I know it wasn't premeditated.* I shake my head with a forgiving sigh, and mutter, "You still set me up."

"I did." Summer beams at my obvious acceptance and links her arm through mine. "Now, let's get this shitty movie over with so we can decide how to get Nate," she says, already pulling me toward the entry.

"Wait!" I pull back on Summer's arm. "I'm not sure I'm ready yet."

Her gaze softens; she knows I'm not talking about the movie. "Those guys were assholes, Cory. I'm not saying you won't ever come across another jerk in your life, but I've never heard a bad thing said about Nate, and at some point you have to trust again, or you'll never find love."

I raise an eyebrow because she needs to do the same thing.

"The love *you* want," she clarifies.

"I'll never understand why *you* don't want it."

Summer shakes her head as an answer. "Cory. You've been pining over Nate for months. It can't hurt to get to know him. Take things at your pace and see what happens."

"What if this time I end up too broken?"

Summer shakes her head in protest. "I will always find a way to put you back together. The only way you're going to know is if you put yourself out there. Now, come on." She loops her arm through mine to lead us inside.

A week later, I find myself standing outside The Ball House. Home to some of the football team. Home to Nate. Don't ask me how I know that. I'm pretty sure everyone does. *Don't they?* With a deep breath, I take in the enormous building that's more like a mansion than a home. My lip's about ready to bust with how hard I'm biting it, and I'm struggling to keep my hands still. Summer stands beside me with a sympathetic smile on her face. She's more enthusiastic than I thought she'd be, but I know I don't have all night. To be honest, I never thought she'd step foot in this place. For good reason...

I take a deep breath and grab Summer's hand. "Okay, I'm ready," I say as my heart continues to race out of my chest.

She smiles and pulls me to the door, pausing for a moment before stepping over the threshold. *Yep, this is harder on her than she's letting on.* I want to focus on that, to ask if she's okay, but a quick scan of my surroundings has my stomach in knots, and I spiral. *Oh, God, what if he turns me down?* I'm definitely not prepared for such a public rejection. I bite the inside of my cheek and stand tall. Well, as tall as I can for my short height, even with my five-inch heels.

It's safe to say I'm on edge until I finally see Nate, and my pulse skyrockets again. *I can't do this.* He doesn't even know who I am. He's going to reject me. He's—

"Relax, it's going to be fine," Summer says, interrupting my freak out.

I shake my head because she's wrong. Just because no one has ever said no to her doesn't mean I'm awarded the same luxury. "I can't do this," I repeat out loud this time.

Summer's eyes widen at something she sees over my shoulder before moving back to me. "How about I help you out?"

"How?"

"I'll be your wing woman. Like Barney Stinson. I'll say *'Have you met Cory?'* then walk away."

I laugh at how ridiculous that sounds, but stop when Summer gives me her 'I'm not joking' look. *Right, okay. I guess that could work.*

I nod, agreeing to her plan because, let's face it, I need her, and then wait patiently while she does her thing. Whatever her thing is. Nervously, I scan the room again. It's easy to see why there are so many people here. *Did someone say eye candy?*

Like Nate, for example. He's a tight end for our college football team and loves a Ball House party. At least, that's what I've heard. I've never been to a party here, because, like I said, Summer's not a fan, and I stay away in support.

Usually.

And really, I only suggested coming here because I thought she'd bail on the deal all together. *No such luck.*

When I finish my visual tour of the room, the first room of many, my eyes land on Summer chatting with a very familiar face. Someone I didn't think she'd ever talk to. I smirk, but then stop when she points my way. *Shit! Is she talking about me and Nate?*

I busy myself by looking at some of the team photos on the wall. When curiosity gets the best of me, I look over to see Dylan, the guy Summer was talking to, walking my way with Nate in tow. *Shit, shit!* Nate's eyes widen, spotting me as Dylan says, "Hey man, I've got a girl I want you to meet," and then walks away without a backwards glance.

Nate recovers from his surprise and smiles. I don't even want to imagine the deer in headlights look I know I currently have.

Taking a deep breath, I somehow smile in return. "Listen, I'm sorry—"

"I'm so glad you're here," he says, and I stop without finishing my sentence. *Huh?*

He laughs and continues. "I... ah..." He grips his shoulder, his smile hesitant. "I wanted to talk to you after catching you the other day. You know, to make sure you're okay after such a terrifying incident."

"I..." *He's joking, Cory.*

Nate's eyes light up with his laugh, and my body relaxes at the sound.

"You're my hero. I don't know what would have happened if it wasn't for you," I sass while fake swooning. Okay, maybe it's not *totally* fake, but mostly.

"I'm glad I could be of service," Nate says with a nod of his head, then offers me his arm like he's straight out of a Jane Austen book. "Can I get you a drink, Cory?" God, is it possible that my fantasies of what Nate would be like are true? I definitely had him pegged as a gentleman.

As we approach the bar, that I hadn't even noticed, he pushes through the crowd while keeping me tucked in close to his side. I relish in the feel of his touch and have to focus hard on *not* turning into a pile of mush. Yep, I'm that girl.

"Can I get a..." Nate looks at me for my order.

I look behind the bartender, aka a freshman, to see my options. "I'd love cider, please."

"Sure thing." Nate nods at something over my head and smiles at me before turning back to order. "A cider, thanks, Jack."

I must give him a puzzled expression because he looks down at me with an apologetic gaze and takes a deep, frustrated breath. "I wasn't lying when I said I was glad you're here. I've wanted to talk to you for a while now." *What?* My heart almost bounces out of my chest. "But..." *And then it drops to the floor with a thud, barely beating.* "...my teammate just reminded me I'm one of the designated drivers tonight. I kind of got caught up in seeing you and forgot."

I inwardly flinch, as my chest tightens. "That's okay, no problem. I'll leave you to it." *As far as escape plans go, it's pretty impressive.* I try to sound upbeat and not let him see the disappointment I'm feeling, but I'm not sure I succeed.

"No, I'm not, ah... what I'm trying to say is that I want time to get to know you. I'm sure I can convince someone to take my place, but I might need to do one last drop off. Will you wait?" *What? Not an escape plan, then?*

I smile, once again hiding my feelings. Relief this time. "Of course. No problem."

"Good." Nate smiles.

"Good." I say back. "Are you needed now? Or..."

"Only if someone asks. At the moment, I'm all yours." He winks, and I'm reminded of the wink he gave me that day in class. And the pain that flashed across his face before it. My brow furrows at the image, but I shake it off.

"I have to say, it's very impressive that you have pre-assigned designated drivers. Very noble of you."

He laughs, but then his face contorts a little. "I wish I could say the tradition started for noble reasons, but it started after an incident we don't really talk about."

I cringe for joking about it and brush my fingers along his arm. "I'm sorry."

"Don't be. It happened; it's over. I'm glad that we do it now, though. At least, I used to be, until you showed up on my designated night."

I feel the heat coating my face as I blush, smiling at his words. This is not how I thought tonight would play out. I guess I'll be thanking Summer later.

We only get a few more minutes together before someone yells from the front door, waving their hand to get his attention. "Nate, you're needed!"

"*Shit!* Duty calls. I'm sorry." I almost laugh at how upset he looks.

"It's okay. I'll be here," I say shyly, hoping he still wants me to stay.

His answering smile tells me everything I need to know. "Perfect. Yes! Thank you. Let me grab your number before I go." He takes down my number before pressing a chaste kiss to my cheek.

And with a quick wave over his shoulder, he dashes off towards the entrance while I stand in a daze, trying to decide if any of that was real.

Chapter Three
Nate

As soon as I've done my drop off, I talk a freshman into taking my place. The Ball House party is as crazy as usual, and while I'd normally be with the boys, I now have other plans. Standing in front of me is the girl I've wanted for months. Yes, months. She's smiling up at me with her beautiful, big, brown-gold eyes and perfect pout, making me want to grip her face, lean down and taste her lips. But I won't. Not yet. I've waited too long to be with this girl. I'm not going to fuck it up.

I don't realize I'm staring until Cory's friend speaks, breaking my trance. "Hi, I'm Summer. Nice to meet you, Nate."

Fuck! Smiling awkwardly, I quickly look at Summer in time to see the hint of a smirk leave her face. "Summer, hi... hi. How are you?" *How are you? Really?*

She smirks again before answering. "I'm great, but I need a drink. Point me in the kitchen's direction?"

"Of course, want me to show you both—"

"Nah, Cory's good for now. I'm a big girl."

I laugh awkwardly, not even sure why I asked that, then direct Summer to the bar before quickly turning my attention back to Cory, locking my eyes with hers.

"Look after my girl," Summer says as I get lost in that amazing brown-gold combo again.

"Always," I say, knowing I mean it. We may have just met, but it's like I have an instinctual desire to always protect her.

Summer whispers something in Cory's ear before walking away.

"Do you want to take a walk?" I ask when we're alone.

Cory smiles shyly and nods. "I'd love to."

"Great, I'll grab a couple of drinks and then we can..." I trail off as I move to grab the ciders I hid on my return. Cory lingers behind, and I hurry to meet back up, gesturing towards the gardens before leading the way.

We walk silently along the garden path. We may look like two friends, but we're practically strangers. It's hard to believe how comfortable it feels. Like we've known each other forever. I'm itching to talk to this girl, really get to know her, but at the same time, I'm happy to just be by her side.

"So... Where are you taking me?" Cory asks, her eyes on the flowers surrounding us.

The Ball House, where I'm currently living, is extremely grand considering the people who live here. There's a huge lagoon style swimming pool, state-of-the-art kitchen, and a mammoth garden that's beautiful and perfectly maintained. By who, that's anyone's guess, but right now, I'll take it.

As we get closer to our destination, my nerves pickup, and I'm suddenly wondering what she'll think. "Just a little further..." I begin, but don't need to say any more because Cory's seen exactly where I'm taking her.

Her eyes trail from the branches of the giant oak tree down to the double swing hanging from one of the thicker limbs, and while I've questioned in the past *why* we have this super romantic spot in the back of a football house yard, Cory's expression alone makes me thankful for its existence.

Her eyes flash to mine with a look of awe and giddiness. "Is it safe?"

"It sure is. I asked one of the guys to test it while I was gone." I wink.

Cory laughs like I'm joking, but I'm really not. I didn't want to chance it breaking when we both sat down.

She sits and grabs the rope before patting the empty spot beside her. I give the swing a slight push before jumping on and turning to face her. Fumbling to find the right words to say, I finally manage, "I brought you here for some privacy. I thought we could play a question game and get to know each other... If you want." *Fuck, I'm nervous. Why am I so nervous?*

"Sure, what type of questions? Just favorite color and stuff like that?"

"I actually mean some deeper questions. I kind of have a few in mind already."

Cory's eyes widen, and a huge smile lights up her face. "You pre-prepared questions?" I nod. I had lots of time to think during my drive. "That's kind of adorable."

I cringe at her words but maintain my smile. *Adorable, really?*

Cory's smile fades and she raises an eyebrow. "Is this the type of game where we remove an item of clothing with each answer we give?" She bats her eyelashes.

My jaw nearly drops. "Ah..." *Is that what she wants?* I didn't think she was like that, but... She suddenly bursts out laughing, and tingles shoot up my thigh as she grips my leg just above the knee.

"Oh, Nate. Sorry, I'm kidding."

"I know," I rasp. I *totally* didn't. "But that brings me to my first question," I continue, still surprised by my reaction to her touch. "Are you the type of girl that *does* get naked on a first date?"

She blanches. "That was your first question?"

"Not even my tenth, but I'm good at thinking on my feet, and well..."

She laughs again and gently slaps my chest with the back of her hand, setting my body alight. Gotta say I'm enjoying every bit of physical affection she throws my way. "Okay, what's your real first question?"

I'm about to answer when she raises her hand between us. "And for the record, no. I'm not that type of girl." She turns away as a beautiful blush colors her skin, but a small smile still plays on her lips. *Good to know.*

"So, my first question is... do you think less of me for not approaching you first?" It's not a get-to-know-you question, but something I need answered.

She turns to me so quickly she almost loses her balance, but I steady her in time. "What do you mean? I thought you were just reacting to Dylan introducing us. You know. Giving it a shot." *What?*

I give her a puzzled expression and she shrugs shyly.

"Cory, I meant what I said. I've wanted to get to know you for a while. Trust me, I've been dying to ask you out. I've just had some stuff going on, and... It's not important. I just wanted to be free of it."

Cory looks down at the ground moving beneath us. "So, my timing sucks."

"No. Definitely not." *Fuck!* "Dylan introducing us was the kick in the ass I needed. I want this. I mean, I came up with questions... This is good. Okay?"

"Okay." She smirks. "So, question two?"

We run through my list of questions and discover we have quite a lot in common, but also a lot that's different. I'm also surprised to learn she knows a hell of a lot about football and has even seen me play. A little buzz goes through me at the thought of her watching me.

We swing for about an hour before making our way back to the party, and as we walk along the path, I reach out to brush her fingers with mine. When she doesn't pull away, I grip her hand and intertwine our fingers, gently pulling her closer. The warmth of her hand in mine sends my pulse racing as realization hits me. *I really like this girl, even more than I thought.*

We spend the next few hours either dancing or hanging out with my friends, and neither of us see Summer again until she waves goodbye and walks away with Dylan's friend, Joel. A perfect match really, seeing as both are only interested in one-night stands. At least, that's what I've heard about Summer.

It's not long after Summer leaves I notice Cory trying to hide a yawn. "Come on, I'll take you home," I say after the fourth one.

"No," she protests, trying to pull me back onto the dance floor, but it's half-hearted, and I can't help but laugh while pulling her into my arms. "Come on. I'm done, too."

I link my hand with hers again as we walk to my car. I may have relinquished my designated driver role, but I only drank two drinks for this very reason. To take Cory home.

The drive to Cory's is peacefully silent, and when we reach her door, the quiet remains, but the tension between us is strong. I've been a gentleman all night, but when she looks up at me with those eyes of hers, I can't wait any longer. I need to feel her lips on mine. Leaning down slowly, I press a soft kiss to her mouth as she sighs.

"Thank you for coming tonight," I say as I kiss her again, unable to resist the touch. It's another chaste kiss because I don't want to push my luck, but when I pull back, I see a hint of disappointment on Cory's face.

"What?" My brow furrows.

She shakes her head with a shy giggle, and it's the most beautiful sound. "Nothing. It's nothing. I had a lovely time."

It's definitely not nothing.

"Cory, please. What is it?"

She blushes and looks up at me through her long fluttering eyelashes, not quite meeting my gaze. "I want you to kiss me like you really want to." Her voice is barely a whisper, but I can feel how much she wants it, and God, I do, too.

Without wasting another second, I grab her face with both hands and slam my lips to hers. She lets out another small giggle, but falls silent when my tongue meets hers and my hands move into her hair. I walk her back slowly until she rests against the wall before deepening the kiss.

Cory's reactive at first, but before long she has one leg wrapped around me, using it to pull my hips into hers, connecting us at the core.

My heart races as a feeling of something new washes over me. It's hard to explain, but it feels like I've been here before. *No, that's not right.* It feels like I've found where I'm meant to be. *Corny as shit? Maybe.* But that doesn't change the fact that there are definitely some intense feelings here.

Cory rocks her hips slightly, and I groan from both pain and pleasure. It feels so good at this moment, but it has to stop.

Sucking on her lips one last time, I somehow release her from my hold and take a step back. "We need to stop right now, or I'll never be able to," I rasp, my breathing erratic. *God, I sound like I just ran a marathon.*

Cory's eyes are wide as she stares up at me. Her chest is rising and falling in time with mine while she bites her lip almost to the point of blood. When she finally speaks, I have to hold back another groan.

"Never stopping works for me," she breathes.

Fuck! "Well, aren't you a firecracker?" I shake my head with a smirk, and I'm rewarded with a beaming smile that lights up her face, as she switches from firecracker to pure sunshine. Maybe she's a little bit of both.

"Ugh! Sorry," she says, shaking her head. "I'm not normally like that." The most beautiful blush sweeps across her skin.

That's why I stopped.

"I know."

Her eyes flash to mine in confusion, and I know she's wondering how, since we've just met. Well, I've liked her for months. I know she's not a sleep-with-a-guy-you-just-met kind of girl. At least, from what I've seen and heard about her. And that's fine by me. I'm more than happy to take this slowly. *Unless I'm wrong.* "Ah, at least, I think I know. You mentioned it on the swing, but even so, you don't strike me as someone who takes things further on the first date."

"Was this a date?" She smirks.

Got me there. "No, absolutely not. Not that tonight wasn't good. Getting to know you was—"

Cory grabs my hand, and the touch silences me as a shiver shoots through my body. *Am I still nervous around this girl?* I just mauled her on her doorstep; we should be past the nervous stage.

She smiles up at me as she squeezes my hand. "You're right about me. So, thank you." She rises to her toes, pressing a kiss to my chin, and I tilt my head enough so our lips can meet instead.

"Can I take you out tomorrow night? For a real first date?" I ask as I pull away and run my hand down her arm, connecting our fingers.

"Yes, perfect. I'd love that." She smiles.

Perfect. I lean in and press my lips to her forehead. "Goodnight, Cory."

"Goodnight, Nate."

I walk away with a smile on my face and a date to plan. I've got a girl to impress.

Chapter Four

Nate

W ho knew planning a date could actually be fun? Hell, who knew the guys would have so many great ideas? You may not believe it, but we've spent Sunday afternoon in the Ball House brainstorming ideas for my date with Cory.

"I think horses should be involved," my teammate, Luke, adds with a very serious expression. "You grew up in a horsey area; shouldn't you show her a piece of your past?"

We all stare at him before bursting out laughing. "A horsey area?" I ask with a raised eyebrow.

"You know what I mean. There were ranches nearby."

"The closest ranch to my family home would have to be at least a hundred miles."

"Close enough." He shrugs, unperturbed by our laughter. "You grew up in a ranchy state."

I roll my eyes and move on to the next good idea. Although, reasons aside, horse riding might actually be a winner.

Cory opens the door with her trademark beaming smile, and I know instantly that tonight is going to be perfect. When I'm finally able to take my eyes off her beautiful face, I run my gaze down her body and have to stop myself from groaning. If this was a cartoon, my eyes would have bulged out of my head.

"Wow. Cory, that outfit... you look..." I clear my throat and mentally snap myself out of my schoolboy persona. "What I'm trying to say is that you look amazing." She's wearing skin-tight jeans and a top that dips low in the front, revealing some spectacular cleavage. It has cut outs at each side, making me itch to place my hands there. To feel her skin beneath my fingertips.

She closes her eyes as a beautiful blush graces her skin before her eyelashes flicker and she looks back at me.

Taking a step forward, I gently cradle her face with my hands and press my lips to hers. She sighs into my mouth, causing my pulse to spike. After a few minutes of making out, I pull away with a smile and link my fingers through hers, taking a deep breath. "Ready to go?" I ask, because if we don't leave now, I'll never be able to move from her doorstep.

* * *

I'm driving with one hand on the steering wheel and the other on Cory's thigh, because of my desperate need to be touching her. This girl is driving me all kinds of crazy, and I don't even think she knows it. I mean, we've only had one night together, if you don't count the months I spent sneaking glances her way, and now I want *all* her nights to be with me. Starting tonight.

First stop on our date agenda is... *drumroll*... horse riding at dusk. *Thank you, Luke.* I was on the phone for an hour before I found somewhere with availability on such short notice, but I had success, and we're now thirty minutes from our destination.

"Are you an animal person, Cory?" I ask out of nowhere. Well, not nowhere for me, but nowhere for her.

She eyes me curiously. "I love most, but—"

Bang!

Cory screams as the back end of the truck slides out of control until I pull us to a stop safely on the side of the road. *What the fuck?*

I turn to Cory to inspect her for any injury. My eyes run from her legs to her face, bouncing all over. "Are you okay?" My heart races as my breathing becomes erratic. *Was that my fault? Did I hit something? My eyes were on the road. Weren't they?*

My hands move involuntarily to Cory's face to assess any damage, not trusting my eyes alone.

"I'm okay, Nate," she says, placing her hands on top of mine. "Are you okay? You're acting a little crazy."

I flinch and pull my hands back, clenching them into fists.

"Sorry. I'm fine. I just... what happened?" I don't let her answer before I jump out of the truck to check. It takes all of two seconds to see the issue. Punctured tire. "*Fuck!*" Thankfully, I've got a spare, but this means we'll be cutting it close for the horse ride.

Cory follows me out to join me at the rear and cringes. "Ouch, that's not good."

"Sorry. This wasn't part of the plan."

"It adds to the adventure." She smiles and drops to a squat beside me. "Can I help? I've changed a few tires in my life."

"Really?" I smile proudly. "This is my first. Care to watch and make sure I'm doing it correctly?"

"Absolutely." She laughs, and a little layer of my stress floats away.

Twenty minutes later, we're on the road again after changing the tire without issue. *Thank God.*

As we get closer to the beach, my nerves kick up a gear. "As much as I would love to keep our first activity as a surprise, I think I need to tell you. You know, in case it's... ah... something that concerns you."

She raises an eyebrow. "That statement is concerning on its own. Why would something on our date worry me? What have you planned?"

I smirk and bite my lip, pretending I'm about to tell her something really out there. "Horseback riding at dusk," I say, scrunching my face, preparing for the worse.

Cory squeals as her hands fly to her mouth, and she turns to face me in her seat. "Really? You better not be messing with me."

I laugh at her response. "I take it that's a good thing?"

"If it's real?" Her face lights up in anticipation and excitement, and I'm reminded of her blinding smile from last night.

"Sure is, Little Bit."

She furrows her brow with a small smile. "Little Bit."

"Yep! You're my little bit of sunshine."

She's quiet then, but when I glance her way, I see the most beautiful smile on her face, highlighted with the hint of a blush.

The rest of the trip runs smoothly, and as soon as we arrive at the beach, Cory is out of the truck, bouncing with energy. The sun is still up in the clouds, preparing for its descent, so we made it in time to get the full dusk effect, and I couldn't be happier.

Linking my fingers with hers, we walk toward the water where the three horses are waiting for us.

Cory pulls me close before we reach them and squeezes my arm. "God, they're so beautiful... And the view... Nate, this is magical."

I press a kiss to her head just as the sky lights up in a flash and the heavens open.

You've got to be kidding me!

A guide reaches for the horses, but when the thunder rolls, one horse rears back, sending us all into a panic. We rush forward to help, grabbing hold of the reins of the calm horses as the owner gets the wild one under control.

She walks our way, horse in tow, with an apologetic smile. "Thank you. I appreciate that. Nate, I presume?" she yells through the rain.

"That's me. Do you need help to get the horses back to the trailer?" I ask, figuring it's safe to assume our trail ride won't be happening.

"Thank you for the offer, but help has arrived." She signals behind us as two teenagers appear out of nowhere, leaving Cory and me free to escape the downpour.

"Don't forget to reschedule!" she calls after us as we run for my truck.

I slam my door closed just as Cory shuts hers. "So, what's next?" she asks with a smirk before bursting out laughing. We're both cold and drenched from the rain, but I don't want this night to be over.

"Dinner?" I shrug before starting the truck and blasting the heating.

"I could definitely eat."

We pull up out the front of a row of shops not far down the road, and I immediately jump out, running around to open Cory's door, knowing I need to salvage some of this night.

Hand in mine, Cory steps out of the truck, her hair plastered to her face, mascara under her eyes, and a stunning smile. She's breathtaking. Literally, I feel my breath hitch.

"Have I told you how beautiful you are?" I whisper before pressing a chaste kiss to her lips. She smiles but doesn't meet my gaze, and I get a sense she's not good at taking compliments.

Gently lifting her chin until her eyes find mine, I brush the wet hair from her face. "You are the most beautiful woman I've ever met."

"Thank you, Nate," Cory replies shyly but shakes her head, almost disbelieving. *Has no one ever said that before?*

I press my lips to hers in another brief kiss before pulling away. "Next stop, your favorite sushi restaurant."

Cory's eyes light up. "You remembered?"

"I remember everything." I wink. "I was going to suggest we have a picnic on the beach, but since..." I wave my hand towards the black sky and heavy rain. "I think we'll eat inside so... *ah shit!*"

We reach the door to find an obnoxious, in your face, closed sign. "What the hell? I called ahead. It's supposed to be open." I turn to Cory in apology. "God, I'm sorry about this... I... are you laughing?"

She's pulled her lips into her mouth, and one of her hands hovers in front of it, trying to hide the evidence, but her eyes give her away. She shakes her head a few times before bursting out in laughter. "Oh, Nate, don't look so sad. The place next door is open."

"It's pizza," I complain. I'm practically pouting, which she clearly finds hilarious.

"I love pizza. Come on." She links her arm through mine and walks me toward the shop, laughing again when we're inside.

She has this ability to make everything feel okay in the world... in me... and I can't quite put my finger on what it is about her. But it's special, that's for sure.

Back in the truck, we eat our pizza and talk. It's no five star sushi, but it's not half bad, and at least the company is nice. The rain falls even heavier, pelting against the roof of the car, and Cory smiles. Tonight, I've discovered that she loves storms. Specifically, she loves listening to them when she's curled up inside under a blanket. The thought of her snuggled up to sleep brings a question to mind.

"What keeps you up at night, Cory?"

Her eyes find mine briefly before turning back to the sky. "Good question." She nods. "Right now, the biggest thing is probably losing my mom."

I swallow a lump in my throat and take her hand in mine. "Is that a possibility?" *Shit!* Of course it is, for everyone. "I mean—"

Cory squeezes my fingers to cut me off. "It was a very real possibility recently, but it's getting better every day. She's in remission for Breast Cancer, and while I should be grateful for that, it still keeps me awake."

"I can imagine, but wow, remission... That's great, Cory. She must be a fighter."

"She's kick ass." She laughs and then shakes her head. "Sorry, that brought down the mood."

"No. God, I want to know everything about you. I love hearing about your family, about anything. Things that keep you awake, things that don't. Things that..." I trail off, not even sure what I'm trying to say.

Cory smiles at my rant. "I'm generally a good sleeper, so that's my main concern, but sometimes... Never mind. What about you?"

My eyebrows pull at her statement. "Never mind? What is it?"

"Are you a good person, Nate?" she asks instead of answering. Or maybe that *is* her answer?

"I... I hope so. At least, I try to be. I'll always try to be. Does that keep you up? Worrying about me?"

"Yes, no, kind of? I just..." She shakes her head again. "I hope you're one of the good ones."

I move so that I'm facing her completely and turn her head so our eyes meet. Her gaze is timid, showing me the true depth of her concern. "I am." *God, I hope that's the truth.*

She nods and smiles. "What keeps you awake, Nate?"

I want to know more about her. About her reasons for possibly doubting me. Instead, I sigh and share my own fears. "Not becoming the person I want to be."

Her brows furrow as she takes in my words. Words that could have many meanings. And for me they do, but... "Put simply, my family has certain expectations for me, and they don't exactly match up with what I want."

"Do they know that?"

"Yes and no. It's not always that simple."

I catch her nod in understanding as another spark of lightning draws my attention. I stare out at the beach in front of me. Ninety percent of the time, it's dark, but when the lightning brightens the sky, I can see the waves crashing at the shoreline. I get why Cory likes it; it's actually quite stunning, but...

"This is not our first date," I say, turning to face Cory again.

Her eyes flash to mine to see if I'm serious. "Oh, it definitely is."

I'm shaking my head before she's even finished talking. "Nope. It's not. I get a do over."

She rolls her eyes and raises her brows in question. "I've had a wonderful time, so I won't be forgetting it... but you can have a do over... If you must."

"I must."

Cory laughs before resting her head on my shoulder and patting my thigh. We watch mother nature's show in comfortable silence until she sighs in contentment and twines our fingers together, squeezing tightly.

"I've had a great time too, Cory," I say after a few minutes. "Spending *any* time with you makes me happy."

"So you agree, this is our—"

"Nope. I still get a do over," I protest, making her laugh again.

Chapter Five

Cory

First date attempt number two. Despite Nate wanting a "do over", I actually had an amazing time on our first date. It may have been a mess, but it was still time spent getting to know each other, and I will never forget that. Ever since officially meeting at the Ball House, we've been almost inseparable, sneaking time in between Nate's football training and our classes, but an actual date has been a couple of weeks in the making. Until now...

The evening breeze hits my cheeks, and I shiver, leaning further into Nate's chest. We're walking down the main street of town after a fantastic dinner and seeing the latest superhero movie, Nate's choice, not mine. He's still raving about some fight scene that I don't even remember. Which is totally his fault, by the way. Because his touch tonight felt different. Possessive. And it was freaking hot...

"Whatcha thinking about?" he asks, giving my shoulder a squeeze.

I feel myself flush pink at the direction my thoughts are heading. "Just about that jerk asking me out while you were getting tickets." *And the way you possessively gripped my waist and crushed your lips to mine when you saw him.*

"That fucker is lucky I didn't punch him. What was he thinking, groping you like that before you'd even answered him?"

I smile shyly as my heart races. Nate may not have turned to violence, but he definitely made it clear I was off limits, both then and through the entire movie. Want to know why I have no idea what happened during the film? It's because Nate's hand was locked on my thigh, on bare skin, just below the hem of my skirt, the skirt that had ridden up rather high when I sat down. Basically, he was inches from my panties. *Who the hell can concentrate with that going on? I mean it, who?*

Nate chuckles beside me, and I freeze momentarily. *Did I say that out loud?* When I look up at him, he's watching me with curious eyes. He's about to say something when a car horn blares, snapping him out of his thoughts.

"I get another do over," he says suddenly, stopping me in my tracks.

"What? Why?" I can't help but laugh at his ridiculously high date expectations.

"For one, I almost punched a guy, and two, I'm pretty sure you hated the movie."

"Ah... No, I didn't... I—"

"Do over." He smirks. "Anyway, here's the truck. Are you ready to go or...?"

When I spot Nate's truck, I want to frown but manage to keep the disappointment off my face. With a quick nod, I walk to the passenger door. I know Nate has some ridiculously early mornings, but I still hate saying goodbye every time I see him.

The drive home is quiet but comfortable, and by the time we pull up out the front of my apartment complex, I'm feeling pretty sleepy.

Nate walks around and opens my door, holding out his hand for me. I let him pull me out and then wrap my arms around his neck before pressing my lips to his.

The kiss is gentle at first but turns frantic pretty quickly. We've been here, in this exact moment, many times before but have never taken it further.

The thought of Nate palming my thigh comes back to me, and I moan into his mouth. Something snaps inside him at the sound, and I'm suddenly lifted into the air and pressed against the truck. I wrap my legs around his waist, clenching my thighs in response.

"Fuck, Cory. You're so goddamn perfect," he says as he curls a hand up into my hair and crushes his lips back to mine.

I moan, rolling my hips to get friction, not even really aware that I'm doing it as Nate groans out loud. I only have to roll my hips three more times before Nate's restraint seems to give, and he grinds up into me, eliciting a groan from us both.

If there was ever a moment to invite him upstairs, this was it. In fact, I'm surprised he hasn't just carried me to the door and demanded I let him in. These aren't the actions of a girl who's scared to take the next step, and yet, that's exactly who I am.

As soon as the negative thoughts hit my brain, I can't unthink them. There are no take backs where this is concerned. The guy groping me in the theater didn't help either. It's like I attract the wrong type of guys. Like I'm a beacon for assholes. *Is Nate going to be one of them?* My body stills, and I grip his shoulders, too far inside my head to keep going. He stops immediately and drops my feet to the ground, leaning his forehead to mine.

We both breathe heavily in silence, trying to control ourselves. He may not even realize he's doing it, but Nate's hands are clenched into fists, like he's physically stopping himself from touching me.

"I'm sorry, I—" I pause, hating that my past relationships are ruining my new one, but not entirely sure what to tell Nate.

His hands relax before moving to my face, and his thumb brushes over my check as he stares into my eyes. "Do not be sorry for wanting to take things slowly. Ever."

"Thank you, but I'm still sorry. I kind of lost control."

Nate smiles, but it's tight. "It happens. It doesn't mean you have to take it further."

"It doesn't happen to you. You don't lose control," I say, hoping he can fill me in on how he was able to stop so quickly. If roles were reversed, and it wasn't my fear getting in the way, I'm not sure I could have done the same.

Nate huffs out a small laugh and shakes his head. "That's not by accident. Trust me."

My brows furrow at his cryptic words, but I mentally shake it off.

He presses his lips to mine one more time and then takes a big step back. "I should go."

I nod, unable to talk, in fear that I'll tell him to stay when I'm not ready. With a wink and a killer smile, Nate runs back around the truck and jumps in.

I've just reached the door to my building when he yells out the open window, "Remember, tonight never happened."

I shake my head and laugh as I walk away.

* * *

A week later I have my head down, staring intently at my book, when I hear the front door click shut. Once again, Summer snuck out without coming to say hi. I know it's because of Nate. Not because she doesn't like him or anything. I think it has more to do with not wanting to be a third wheel, or feeling like she'd be intruding on our time together.

Yes, I've been spending all my time with Nate. Does that mean I've neglected my relationship with Summer a little? Yes. Will she forgive me? Definitely, yes. But that's no excuse. We're both being crappy friends at the moment, and one of us needs to fix this.

The door rattles again, signaling Summer's return. *Here's my chance.* Jumping up from the couch, I run to the door to meet her as she walks back in.

"Hi!"

"Jesus, Cory." She jumps as her hand goes to her heart. *Oops.*

"Sorry, I just. I haven't seen you in a while, and I didn't want to miss you."

She crinkles her nose and offers me an apologetic smile. "No, I'm sorry. Now's not the best time. I really need to get to class. I just came back to get my phone." She walks over to the counter to collect said phone and then moves back to the door.

"Oh, of course," I say, putting on my best all-is-fine smile. "No problem. Let's organize something soon. I'll message you."

"Sounds great. Love you." With a quick wave, she walks away.

"Love you, too," I say to an empty hallway as I shut the door.

I don't actually blame her for distancing herself; there are a number of valid reasons she might be doing it, but I could really use a friend.

Not that things aren't great with Nate, because they are. But I could really use some of Summer's badass, confident attitude, as well as her no bullshit, say-it-like-it-is view of the world. Specifically, I need her to tell me to get out of my head in certain parts of my relationship.

My phone buzzes, snapping me out of my thoughts, and I realize I'm still standing at the door. I smile when I see Nate's name on the screen.

Nate: Training kicked my ass this morning, but the thought of seeing you tonight is getting me through.

My heart races as I read his words and almost beats out of my chest when I picture him texting me after practice, all sweaty and hot. *Ugh! How long is it before it's tonight?* It's now been three weeks since we got together, and despite not having had a first date, according to Nate, things between us couldn't be better. Actually, that's a lie, they could definitely be better. But that's on me and *my* issues, not him.

Every time we come close to... you know, I freak out. We've been doing other stuff, amazing stuff, but the actual act... I can't bring myself to take that next step. I know the exact reason why, and it's bullshit. Unfortunately, my mind goes straight into panic mode whenever things start to move in that direction. When we get intimate. When things heat up, and... *Sex. It's sex, Cory.* That's what I'm struggling with. Geez, no wonder I'm not doing it if I can't even say the word.

Nate's been amazing, but I can tell he's having a hard time holding back for me. I smile at the memory of him pressing me against his truck after our latest date fail and curse my insecurities. We've had a few heated moments since that day but still haven't gone all the way. I know Nate's a good guy and nothing like my ex-boyfriends, but I still can't seem to take that next step. Like it's only a matter of time. After all, my exes were great, too, until they weren't...

Tonight, Nate's cooking me dinner at my place, because, apparently, he's an amazing cook, *his words not mine.* He wants to wow me with his skills and win me over with my tastebuds, *again, his words.* It's the first time we'll have a full night together, and I have to admit the thought of being alone has filled me with a mix of nervous and excited energy. Nate's been over before. In fact, he's almost a regular. But it's usually between classes or a lazy Sunday afternoon. This feels different. In a good way.

I fill my day with housework and studying, since Friday is my only class-free day, and then sit on the couch staring at the TV until the sun sets and Nate finally arrives.

"That's a lot of bags," I say, looking at his full hands. "I know I can't cook to save myself, but do you really think we wouldn't have utensils?" I laugh as Nate places a wooden spoon on the counter.

He stares at me intently before pulling open what is typically the utensil drawer. "You're right. Can you grab yours for me?" he says, picking up the spoon and waving it in the air.

His eyes follow my every move as I peer into the drawer. The confident smirk tells me I won't find what he's asking for. I can't help but laugh at just how lacking our kitchen actually is. *How the hell do we survive?* "Okay, smartass. I'm guessing you took the time to check what you'd need to bring."

"Always be prepared, Cory," he says, tapping his temple. "Especially when you want to impress someone."

I bite my lip as a giddy feeling takes over. "Are you still trying to do that? Impress me, I mean?"

"Yep. And I have no plans to *ever* stop," he says, his focus now on unpacking the food. Like his words are no big deal. Meanwhile, my romantic heart is swooning.

Watching Nate cook is a lot sexier than I was prepared for. In fact, the thought never even crossed my mind. But the way he looks up at me with a small smile while mixing the ingredients, or bites his lip in concentration, has me struggling to keep my hands to myself.

When the timer goes off for the sauce, Nate holds the spoon out for me to try. We're having a seafood pasta that already smells amazing, and I can't wait to devour it, *among other things*. I lean forward to wrap my lips around the spoon, but he meets me with his mouth instead.

The spoon drops to the floor and things turn frantic as Nate grips my face, groaning into my mouth. I grab his shirt and pull him closer, walking backwards until my back hits the fridge, and he's pushing against me. He moves one hand from my face to my breast, and I cry out when he squeezes before rubbing a finger over my nipple. *Heaven. This is heaven. This* I'm okay with. I'm about to wrap a leg around his waist when a second timer goes off.

Nate pulls back quickly but doesn't move away; instead, he stares at me as he catches his breath. I bite my lip at the look of pure lust in his eyes, and he leans forward to pull it free, using his teeth.

My eyes widen in excitement at the move, but before I can take things further, he breaks away and continues with his dinner preparations.

Tease. I shake my head, trying to hide my smile, when a tiny smirk appears on his face. He knows exactly what he's doing to me.

Ten minutes later, we're sitting across from one another, eating one of the most delicious meals I've ever had cooked for me, and all I can think about is Nate. More specifically, how far I'm willing to go tonight. He smirks and raises an eyebrow as if reading my thoughts and then shakes his head, no doubt to rid himself of whatever image he conjured.

We've just finished dinner when Nate's phone rings and I welcome the distraction so I can take a minute to myself. "You should get that. I'm just going to the bathroom."

"Oh, that's okay. I—"

"It's fine, Nate. I'll be back." I smile and head out of the room.

As soon as I'm in the bathroom, I take a deep breath and smile. Tonight has been amazing, beyond amazing. Everything feels so easy with Nate. We just...*click*. I want to take things to the next level. Desperately. But I just never know when my fears are going to creep in.

I do what I need to in the bathroom and then take another deep breath before leaving. I can't hear Nate talking as I walk toward him, so I assume he either didn't take the call or hung up. I'm about to ask him when he suddenly speaks.

"I know; I'm sorry. It would be great to catch up with everyone, but the timing isn't good."

He pauses, presumably listening to a response, and smiles when he sees me enter the room. "Yeah. Yeah. I get it. I'll try harder. I promise."

He's quiet again, and then his tone changes. "Come on. You can't say that anymore."

He grabs my hand and links our fingers, pulling me down to straddle his lap. He puts the call on speaker and sets the phone down so he can wrap both arms around me.

I'm about to plant a kiss on my man's mouth when a female voice draws my attention. "Which part? The 'I miss you' or the 'babe'? We've always said that to one another. What's the big deal?" *What?*

"Things are different now. I gotta go, but I'll call you soon."

Nate hangs up and sighs. "I'm sorry about that. She can talk, that one."

And who exactly is she, Nate? I need to know.

I smile. "It's okay. Not like I was waiting long." *Who was it?* "So, is it finally time for dessert?" I ask, changing the subject.

I move to get up, but he pulls me back down. "That was Liv. She's a family friend that I... ah... dated for a while. I've known her for a long time. You can ask me anything, Cory. Whatever questions you have. I'll never lie to you."

I suck in a breath as my fears race to the surface. *Does he want her back? She's still calling, so maybe he does. Or shit! Are they still together? Oh, God, it's happening again.*

"Woah! You're spiraling. I can see it." He grabs my face and forces me to look at him. "There's nothing going on with Liv. We've been over for a while. We're just friends."

My chest feels tight as I consider his words. My eyes bounce between his, but I'm not entirely sure what I'm looking for.

"I promise." Nate says, and the sincerity he displays has my heart pounding and my body moving forward to connect our lips. Anything to rid myself of these thoughts. *And maybe show him I'm the better option. No, stop it.*

Nate groans at the contact and immediately grips my face harder before sliding one hand into my hair, his go-to move that always has me weak in the knees.

It doesn't take long before we're both moving against each other, trying to seek the friction we desperately need. Nate's so hard beneath me that every thrust has me teetering on the edge of release, but not quite close enough to go over.

When his hands move from my face to my waist to pull me more forcefully against him, I cry out in pleasure. *God, I'm so close; if I could just...*

Nate's hand moves to my thighs before slipping underneath my skirt. The anticipation of his touch has me so worked up, I almost grab his wrist to move him to where I want him, but I don't need to. He knows.

I hold my breath, gripping Nate's shirt as he moves my panties to the side and runs a finger along my core. "Fuck, Cory. I..." he trails off with a groan as he dips a finger inside me and rubs me at the same time. It's too much for me to handle. I want it to last longer, but tonight's been one long session of foreplay and, "Yes! Nate. Yes." My entire body tightens as I explode around him. He grunts a few curse words before smothering my cries of pleasure with a bruising kiss.

The second my body stops pulsing and I can see straight, I slide my ass backwards and reach for the button on Nate's jeans, sucking on his neck as I go. "Cory, Fuck. No, please. Yes."

What is he asking? My mind is too hazy to understand.

With the zip down, I slip my hand inside and massage his length. When I realize I'm not getting anywhere this way, I stand and pull him to his feet before dropping to the floor in front of him.

"Oh, Fuuuck!" Nate groans and grabs my face in his hands. "Wait! Not like this; I want to be inside you. I need..."

I freeze at his words while, at the same time, a pulse runs straight to my core in anticipation. My mind and body are completely at odds as to what I want. I try to ignore my mind, to take what my body so desperately seeks, but I can't.

"Nate, I'm sorry..." My head drops, and my eyes well with tears. *Why can't I do this?*

"Hey. No." Nate says, gently lifting my chin with his index finger until my eyes meet his. "How many times do I have to tell you? I'll wait."

He starts to lower himself to the floor to be level with me, but I stop him and wrap my lips around his length. "Argh! Shit," he yells out, not expecting my attack. "Cory, no. You don't need to... Ah, fuck."

He tries to pull out of my mouth, but I grip his ass and pull him into me, working him to the point of no return. His breaths become ragged, and I love the feeling I get knowing he's under my control.

He falls to a heap on the floor in front of me as soon as he's found his release, and then pulls me into a crushing hug. "You did *not* have to do that. But God, was it good."

I giggle, then rise, pulling him up with me and walking him toward my bedroom. "Will you stay?" I ask. "To sleep?"

A nervous expression briefly crosses his face, but he smiles and nods, following me inside.

* * *

After another heavy make-out session in the morning, Nate left for a run with the guys from his team.

I'm a morning person, so I get up and start my day not long after he's gone.

It's hours later before Summer comes moping into the room, looking worse for wear.

"Big night?" I ask, even though I know the answer. I heard her talking to Nate in the early hours of morning when she was just getting home.

"Big? No. Late? Yes." She heads straight for the coffee I prepared earlier and pours herself a cup. "As you know, I ran into Nate this morning."

"And..." I raise an eyebrow and smirk.

"And he stayed over?" She says it like a question, but that's not really what she's asking.

"Yes, he stayed over."

"That's great, Cory. I know that's a big deal for you, and I'm sorry I haven't been here—"

"Oh, we haven't... we didn't." I interrupt, but then cut myself off.

Summer's brows furrow in confusion, but she recovers quickly. "Sorry, Nate said something... Never mind. Are you still worried about him? He's a good one, Cory."

"I know. I know! I just can't seem to get past the bullshit in my head. I heard what Nate said to you, and he was alluding to us doing *other* things, not the actual thing." I smirk but also feel myself blush.

Summer laughs and is about to say more, but I cut her off, not wanting to talk about it. Before last night, I would have wanted to spill every last detail. But now, I'm just embarrassed that I can't seem to get my shit together.

"I'm sure I'll get there," I say with a smile. "I just need to keep telling myself that, like you said, he's a good one." *I hope. Thoughts of his ex-girlfriend come to mind, but I push them back down.* "Anyway, let's move on."

"Okay," Summer says with a frown. Despite me thinking she'd be glad to avoid a deep conversation, based on her recent disappearing act, she actually seems a little reluctant to drop it, so I change the subject just in time for Nate to return for our Sunday movie afternoon.

Chapter Six

Nate

For the next two weeks, Cory and I have many sleepovers but never get further than third base. I wish she would talk to me about her reasons so I can help. But in the meantime, I can't say I'm not satisfied, because I am. Gotta say, life with Cory is pretty damn good. Well, except for right now.

Right now, I want to throw up. It's our first date. Ever. The only one we've had, *in my book*, and instead of it being a positive experience, I'm staring up at a tall structure in front of me with my heart in my throat. I can't for the life of me figure out why I agreed to this insanity, but here we are. *Maybe because you love her.* Fuck! My eyes shoot to Cory's as I let that sink in. *Do I love her?* I do. Of course, I love her. If I'm being completely honest with myself, I'd say I've loved her for weeks.

I love her. I love her. I love her. I run the words over and over in my head, testing them out. I'm momentarily distracted until soft fingers brush mine and the warmth of Cory's hand grips me. "I've changed my mind. We don't have to do this," she says as she wraps her small body around my much larger one.

I smile down at her and find myself surprised that it's not forced. For some reason, I feel stronger with her by my side. *Because you love her.* "Let's get it over with," I say. I can do this.

Cory lets out a small squeal as I pull her forward. When she found out about my very specific phobia last week, thanks to Dylan, she insisted we attend the local summer fair and each have a go at facing our fears, hers being the Haunted House. I agreed immediately because, well, everyone was staring at me, and I didn't want to let her down. But now, I'm definitely regretting it.

We reach the bottom of the Ferris Wheel, and my pulse spikes. Yep, I said what I said... Ferris Wheel. That's what has me tied up in knots, and it has nothing to do with having a fear of heights. There's just something about leaving my life in the hands of a clunky old machine that sways in the air while being controlled by some dude that really doesn't want to be here. It freaks me out.

Fortunately, or maybe unfortunately, the line moves quickly, and before I know it, I'm being directed into a carriage. As soon as we're seated, Cory grips my hand tightly, giving it a quick squeeze before leaning into me. *Is that allowed? Is she going to throw our weight distribution off?* I try to smile at her, but she laughs at how fake it is.

Despite my heart beating out of my chest and the sweat threatening to drip down my forehead, the beginning of the ride is okay. Nice even. Cory sings, 'Wherever You Will Go' by The Calling, quietly beside me, as we take in the stunning views. Her hand never once leaves mine. When we stop at the top, I know it's all part of the procedure and hold back my panic. At least, I try to, until we jolt slightly and then stop again. I grip the bar in front of me and take a deep breath. *It's okay. I'm fine. We're all fine.*

"We're going to die! We're all going to die!" A young girl screams in the carriage behind us.

Fuck! I am not fine.

"Oh shit!" Cory says, covering her mouth to hide her laugh. "You're okay, Nate. It's okay." She rubs the hand I have locked around the safety bar, trying to calm me, but there's no chance in hell that's happening.

Taking deep breaths, I bark out an "easy for you to say," while closing my eyes and counting to ten.

One Mississippi... Two Mississippi... Three—

Cory's hand lands on my leg, higher than one would deem appropriate for a kid's ride, and then moves its way up. I inhale a sharp breath and focus on her touch as she runs her palm close to my growing hardness before moving back down.

Calming slightly, I open my eyes, following the path of her movement with my gaze. My heart rate spikes again as the anticipation of her touch sends my pulse into overdrive. "Fuck, Cory." *Isn't this something that only happens in the movies?*

On her third route, she doesn't stop. Instead, she works her hand back and forth, almost gripping my length over my shorts. If I don't concentrate, I'm going to make a mess in approximately five seconds. "Cory," I rasp. "You have to stop."

She doesn't.

"Cory, please. *Fuck.*" My voice is strained and breathy, but loud enough that she hears it and stops just as the crowd below comes into view.

"You did it!" she yells excitedly as we come to a stop on the ground, and I can't help the laugh that escapes me. This girl is really something.

I did it. I survived.

I even consider begging the Carnie to give us another ride, so I can fix my current situation, but decide it's not worth it. It's dark. If someone can tell I'm hard, then it's lucky for them.

I adjust myself as I walk toward the exit and smile at Cory's sweet giggles beside me. "That wasn't so bad, was it?"

"It was awful. On so many levels." *Not a lie.* It was terrifying up there, and now I'm frustrated down here. "Your turn, Little

Bit." I say to Cory and watch the blood drain from her face. *Shit.* That's the first time she hasn't smiled at her nickname. She must be terrified. I could never put her through the fear I just felt. "Actually, I've changed my mind. I need you home. *Now.*"

Her eyes spring to mine and widen as she recognizes my ploy for what it is. "Oh, Nate, thank you, but I can do this."

I wrap my arms around her waist and lift her into the air, pressing our lips together in a passionate kiss. Our tongues swirl as Cory's arms lock around my neck, pulling me closer. "Let's go home," I say against her mouth, and this time I mean it for the implied reason.

Cory wriggles out of my grip and drops her feet to the ground. "Nope, I'm doing it." My tough Little Bit. *How did I get this girl again?*

Shoulders high, full of confidence, she moves her sweet ass towards the Haunted House without looking back. I jog to catch up to her and take her hand in mine. She's a determined little thing when she wants to be.

We're almost there when she stops suddenly, frozen in place. I turn to offer her a reassuring smile, but she's not looking toward the screams. No, her pale face and wide eyes are directed at a guy walking toward us.

Something doesn't feel right, so I maneuver my body until I'm slightly in front of her and widen my stance. Cory's grip on my hand tightens, telling me my instincts are right; this guy means trouble.

"Cory Walton? It's been a long time. How are you?" He cups her shoulder with his palm and looks down at her with a smile, completely ignoring my existence.

Cory shakes him off. "Never better, thanks. This is Nate, my boyfriend."

The guy acknowledges me for the first time, giving me a nod before looking back at Cory. *Who the fuck does he think he is? And more to the point, who the fuck is he?*

"Glad to see you're not still hung up on our situation. It hit you harder than I thought it would. Honestly, I thought you knew. Anyway, I didn't come over to rehash the past. I wanted to tell you, you're looking hot as fuck these days, and if you change your mind about *things*, you know where to find me." *Is he for real?*

I take a step forward, clenching my fist. I'm about to teach this guy some manners when Cory grabs my wrist and pulls it back toward her.

She steps in front of me, like she's my protector, and straightens her shoulders, trying to appear confident. Actually, that's not fair. She looks confident to the outside world. But inside, I know she's not feeling it at all by the way her hand was trembling when she touched me, and I'm close enough to have heard the hitch in her breath.

She looks the guy square in the eye and scoffs. "You thought I knew? Are you kidding me? You know what? Never mind. I won't be changing my mind. Ever. So please, don't bother approaching me if you see me in the future. I'm done."

With that, she turns and walks away, but not before linking our fingers and pulling me along. I want to cheer. I want to tell her I'm proud of her. Hell, I want to ask her what the conversation was even about. But I don't do any of that. I follow her silently, giving her the time and space to work through whatever just happened. Because make no mistake, fake confidence aside, that exchange hurt her. I could see it written all over her face and it has me clenching my fist at the thought.

When we're out of his sight, Cory stops before throwing herself into my arms. She's shaking slightly, so I pull her in close and rock her from side to side, kissing the top of her head. "I've got you. Are you okay?"

She looks up at me with beautiful, albeit weary, eyes and smiles. "I will be. That was... actually, I'd rather not get into it here if that's okay?"

I nod and then pull her toward the exit. We're done here.

"Where are you going?" she asks, digging her feet into the ground.

I turn to her with a puzzled expression. "I'm taking you home. Where else would we be going?"

"Ah, to the Haunted House." She gives my hand a tug before letting go and walking back in the direction of the rides.

All I can do is shake my head and laugh.

❖ ❖ ❖

Just like the Ferris Wheel, the line's short. *We obviously came on a good day.* When we head inside, it takes all of two seconds in the darkness for Cory to scream... and for me to realize this was a bad idea. One of the worst she's ever had. With me anyway.

After about fifteen hair raising screams, fourteen from Cory and one from me, we've had enough. Or at least, Cory has. I bend down and tell her to jump on my back, racing us through the end of the maze. The sooner we get this done the better, and we're so close I can actually smell the fresh air. *We've made it.*

With a few feet to go, Cory screams out and tightens her hold on me. She thrashes around slightly and then drops off my back. *What the...*

"Get the hell away from me," she cries out, taking a step back. There's just enough light to see a man dressed as Leatherface standing inappropriately close to my girl. Suddenly, all I see is red. *What. The. Fuck!*

I move faster than I ever have on the field, and before I know it, I have Leatherface pinned against the wall, and my fist inches from meeting his face. His eyes widen, and his chainsaw falls to the ground with a clang. "What did you do to her?" I yell as I prepare to punch him in the nose. "Tell me, asshole!"

On some level, I know I shouldn't be so aggressive, but I won't let someone else get away with this. My mind flashes between Cory's scared face and the bruised face of my mother as I prepare to rearrange his.

"Nate!" Cory screams, stopping me in my tracks. She grabs my hands and drags me toward the door as fast as her little legs will take her. I want to go back, desperate to teach him a lesson, but I don't.

When we break out into the open air, we move quickly, until we're far enough away from that nightmare, and then we both stare at each other in silence, breathing rapidly.

Cory's the first to break as a laugh bursts out of her. I quickly follow with a laugh of my own, but it's more of a nervous reaction. "What just happened?" I ask with a smile.

"You got yourself kicked out of the fair; that's what," someone says from behind us, freezing us in place. "You're lucky that's the worst that's going to happen."

I don't argue or even look at the person who owns the voice. Instead, I grip Cory's hand tightly in mine and power walk toward the exit. We've just reached the gate when Cory looks at me with mischief in her gaze. "Tonight never happened, right?"

I can't stop the laugh that bursts out of me. "Correct. Do over," I say as I press a kiss to her cheek and lead her away from the madness.

We take our time walking home after our third date fail and enjoy the comfortable silence. I calm myself down, faster than I thought I would, but still have a sick feeling in my stomach. I hate the thought of anyone getting away with assault. My mother ended up... *Ugh!* I can't let that get to me. I need to focus on something else or I'm going to get angry again.

When we pass by a playground, Cory wanders in, pulling me along with her. *This will do.* She lets go of my hand when we reach the swings and sits down, leaning back to look up at the sky.

The moonlight shines brightly on her skin, and her eyes twinkle like the stars. Her long hair falls down toward the ground and dances around with the welcomed breeze. I've never seen anything more perfect in my life.

She sits up again and pushes off the ground to put the swing in motion until I step in behind her, and take over the movement, gently pushing her through the air.

The moment reminds me of the night we first got to know each other, and I can't help but smile at how far we've come. It honestly feels like we've been in each other's lives forever, even though it's been less than two months.

I know why I did it, but I can't believe I wasted so much time thinking about her without ever making a move. This girl has fast become my world, my *everything*. My heart spikes at the thought of spending forever with Cory, and a warmth I've never felt before takes over me.

I slow the swing and pull it to a stop. Cory lays back to look at me over her shoulder, and I stare down at her in awe. *I know I'm in love with her, but this feels like something bigger.*

Leaning down, I take her lips in mine, gripping the swing to keep her from falling. She sighs into my mouth and then opens hers so I can slip in my tongue.

Cory sucks my tongue further into her mouth and moans when one of my hands grips her jaw to deepen the kiss. A kiss that is slow and passionate and full of emotion. When we're both almost out of breath, she breaks away and rises to her feet. "You, Nate Edwards, are an excellent kisser."

I smile and walk to the front of the swing, pulling her up to standing. I brush a hair away from her face and press my lips to hers once more. My heart pounds so hard, I'm surprised it's not moving my shirt. "Cory," I rasp. "I'm so fucking in love with you I can't see straight."

She laughs nervously and buries her nose into my chest before mumbling something back.

"Sorry, I didn't catch that."

She pulls back and looks into my eyes. And my soul. Her cheeks are flushed, and I'm not sure if it's leftover from our passionate kiss or if she's embarrassed about something. I'm about to ask when she says, "I'm so fucking in love with you, too."

My heart cracks in two at her words, and I'm ready to hand over the half that now belongs to her.

I smile, pressing a kiss to her forehead, and sway her back and forth to the non-existent music. We stay like that until Cory looks up at me through her long lashes. "Take me home, Nate."

Her words are simple, but combined with her expression, I see the deeper meaning.

Tonight's the night.

As we walk home, I smile at the memory of her confession and suddenly realize the reason for her embarrassment. That's the first time she's said *fuck* around me, and that makes it so much more meaningful.

When we get back to Cory's place, Summer isn't home, which shouldn't surprise me, considering it's a Saturday night. I walk straight into the kitchen, making myself at home. "Can I get you a drink?" I ask, helping myself to the contents of the fridge. Cory shakes her head and eyes me curiously. Like I'm acting strange. Am I?

Her expression quickly turns to one of lust, and I swallow a lump in my throat, suddenly nervous. Or maybe not so suddenly. We've fooled around before. That look in her eyes isn't anything new, and yet... it is. I knew what she wanted the second she asked me to take her home. The question is... why does that make me nervous?

Maybe it's because we said I love you and everything feels deeper, or maybe it's because I almost tore apart two people tonight and I'm still feeling possessive. For whatever reason, instead of doing what we both want, I try to slow down and say, "Want to watch a movie, or listen to music, or—"

Cory cuts me off by launching herself at me and crashing her lips to mine.

"Or this," I mumble against her mouth. "We can definitely do this." Okay, so this isn't slow, but it's so much better.

Cory laughs as I pick her up honeymoon style and carry her to her room. Once inside, I pull away before lowering her feet to the ground and taking a step back. "I want to do this right and go at your pace. Just tell me what you want."

She smiles before her expression turns serious. "I want you. Now," she rasps and then lifts her top over her head to reveal a black lace bra underneath. I swallow as I blatantly check her out. "Fuck, you're beautiful," I say, wanting nothing more than to devour her.

Cory reaches for the button of her jeans but takes her time, giving me a chance to take over. I'm focused on her hands, torn between wanting to help and wanting to watch the show. But when the zip makes its way down, offering me a sneak peek at her panties, the need to touch her wins out.

I reach over and remove her hands, replacing them with mine. I take my time sliding the jeans down her legs, placing kisses on her stomach and thighs as I go. Cory watches my every move, looking like she wants to eat me. *Fuck, it's hot.*

I kiss my way back up her legs and then lift her up again, lowering her onto the bed. She pouts, and I can't help but laugh at her expression. "If you touch me the way I just touched you, this will be over really quickly."

She laughs and motions for me to get a move on and then bites her lip as I strip off my clothes.

When I'm naked in front of her, I pause and stare down at her gorgeous body before meeting her eyes. "Tell me what you want, Cory."

Without saying a word, she slides her panties down and opens her legs in invitation.

"Fuck!" I groan at the sight in front of me as my heart beats out of my chest. I don't dare waste another minute, quickly sheathing myself and lowering on top of her. When we're almost completely connected, I stop and hold my weight above her.

"I won't break," she says, giving me a warm smile. I know she won't. It's not her I'm worried about.

"But I might," I rasp out, trying to hide how intense my feelings are right now.

Cory laughs and pulls me down until we're flush, wrapping her legs around me before devouring my mouth. *Well, okay then.* We rub against each other, working ourselves into a frenzy, until I finally line myself up with her core and press gently inside.

Holy Fuck!

I'm met with slight resistance when I thrust, and though I know Cory's not a virgin, this has to be hurting her. "God, Cory, you're so tight, and I'm hurting you. Do you want me to stop?"

"Don't stop," she moans, and I do as she says, attempting to push in a little further with each move. On the fourth try, I make it all the way, and it feels too good to be real. I pause to allow Cory, and maybe me, time to adjust as she cries out in pleasure. "God. Oh, God."

God? I wish. "Nah, it's just me. Are you good for me to move?" *Please be good for me to move.*

She huffs out a laugh and then moans when I twitch inside her. "God, please, yesss," she practically screams, and the sound is the final straw.

I start off slow, terrified of hurting her, but then increase the speed and intensity as I whisper compliments in her ear. "You're perfect." "You feel so good." "I will never forget this."

It's not long before her body quivers, almost ready to explode. I change the angle of my hips to create a new sensation, and when she lifts her hips to match my thrusts, I slide deeper inside her, biting my tongue to maintain control.

When I rub my thumb over Cory's nipple, she screams out her release and then collapses back onto the pillows.

My eyes roll into the back of my head, and a groan rips from within me as I follow her over the edge. When I've emptied myself inside her, I fall onto the bed by her side and grab her hand. "Thank you," I joke and am rewarded with the most beautiful giggle.

"No, thank *you*," she replies and then curls her body into mine. "That was really something, huh?" she asks softly. Her voice quivers a little with nerves.

I have to disagree with her on that; it was so much more than something. I pull her closer and press a kiss to her forehead before whispering.

"No, Cory. That was *everything*."

Chapter Seven

Cory

"Do you have to be so happy all the time?" Summer asks from her relaxed position where she's reading on the couch. She's lying down with her head on the armrest and her legs up on the back of the two-seater. I laugh when she peers up at me over the top of her book with a small smirk. We've finally been spending more time together and everything feels whole again.

She's right. I am happy. All. The. Time. And why wouldn't I be? Classes are good. The weather is beautiful. I'm surrounded by wonderful friends and family. Oh, and... I have Nate. My beautiful, caring, sexy, passionate boyfriend, Nate. I guess there's that, too. I've been floating on cloud nine since the day of the carnival and often replay the moment he said I love you over and over in my mind.

Summer shakes her head at me as if reading my thoughts, and I poke my tongue out in response. "What?" I ask. "You could be happy, too, you know."

She narrows her eyes at me as her smile drops. Ugh, I wish she wasn't so closed off when it comes to love. It kills me that she has this great guy standing right in front of her, but she's oblivious. No, that's not true; she flat out ignores his feelings towards her. And any she has for him, for that matter.

"Enough," she says. "I can see your mind working, and I don't want to hear it." She smirks again, but this one doesn't have the same sass to it. "What time are you heading to Nate's? He's got his first game tomorrow, right?" Now, it's my turn to smirk because while she won't ever admit it, that right there is more proof that she's definitely hung up on a certain football player. Why else would she know the schedule?

"It's on the calendar," she says, as if reading my thoughts again, the tone of her voice telling me she's mentally rolling her eyes.

I laugh as a knock on the door interrupts my chance at saying anything back. Speaking of football players... *There's my man.* I bounce over to the door just to mess with Summer and laugh when she rolls her eyes for real this time.

When I throw back the door, Nate's standing in the hall, looking a little disheveled. His eyes are slightly bloodshot, like he's been rubbing them, or not sleeping, and his usual warm smile has been replaced with a fake one.

"Nate? Is everything okay?" Stupid question, because clearly it's not, but it's out there, so I let it hang in the air.

He squeezes his eyes shut before opening them again, breaking out of his trance. "Are you ready to go?" *Okay, ignore the question.*

"Yes, of course. Let's go."

I step into the kitchen to grab my bag, noticing Summer's eyes on mine. She raises an eyebrow in question when I look her way. *I wish I knew, Summer, but I don't.* I shrug my shoulders and walk away, not wanting to analyze her concerned expression.

The drive to Nate's is quiet except for the soft tones of the radio. 'Ain't No Sunshine' by Bill Withers plays through the speakers, pulling me from my thoughts. It's the type of song that Nate would normally sing along to, but right now, he's dead silent, and that's not a good sign. *What the hell is going on?*

When we arrive, Nate heads straight to his room, and I follow. He holds the door open for me as I enter and then closes it behind himself. A heavy lump forms in my chest. *He's breaking up with me. I don't know why, and I'm completely blindsided, but he's definitely breaking up with me.*

"I don't want to break up," I blurt, dropping onto the bed with my eyes directed at the floor.

"Shit, Cory. God. Fuck. That's not..." Nate sits down beside me and wraps his arms around my body. "I definitely don't want to break up." *But... I feel a but.* "Please, hear me out before you say anything."

So much worse than a but.

I look up into his eyes, and all I see is apprehension staring back at me. *What is going on?* My heart rate spikes, and I bite my cheek to keep my emotions at bay. He looks away as he speaks. "My family's here for my first game. My parents and my sister."

"Nate that's—"

"They've asked for my allocated seats," he says, cutting me off. My shoulders sag in relief at his words. *Is that all he's worried about? I don't mind sitting with them. Or somewhere else. God, why would—*

"My ex came with them."

What?

Nate's eyes focus on the floor while his hands clench into fists on his knees, bouncing nervously. He takes a deep breath and looks up at me with an expression I can't quite decipher. "I promise you I didn't invite her. I didn't invite any of them. They came to surprise me, and she came, too."

He's clearly anxious about this for a reason that I'm not seeing. He told me there was nothing to worry about when it came to her, so I don't understand. "I believe you, but I need to know... Why are you so worked up about it?"

Nate looks away guiltily and squeezes his eyes shut. When he opens them again, they shine with apology. "I need you to know this changes nothing between us."

I'm taken aback by his words, feeling myself pulling away from him. "Then why are you so worried?" I ask nervously. Whatever he'sabout to say can't be good.

"Because, while I had *nothing* to do with it, I'm not sure how you're going to take what I'm about to say and I can't lose you," he stresses, his eyes boring into me earnestly.

"Cory, I love you more than I ever thought I could love someone else. You're the girl I'm going to marry. Have kids with. I know that. I've known that for a while."

A lump forms in my throat as I hold back some tears. "Then why would you lose me? What are you hiding that might make me walk away?"

He stands and paces the room. It's then that I notice the mess. His usually tidy room looks ransacked. As much as I want to ask about it, I don't interrupt him. Emotions run wild on his face until he settles on anger.

"My parents think my ex and I are back together." Ah, *what?*

I don't speak. I don't even react at all. I'm not sure what I'm meant to say. That's bad, but it's an easy fix, right?

"And it needs to stay that way, for now."

My eyes widen and flash to him in confusion. *Did he just say...?* "Um, sorry, I thought you just said—"

"I did," he rasps. "I'm so fucking sorry, Cory. I'm not entirely sure of her reason yet, but Liv told my parents we got back together last week and then begged them to come to my game today. She's been through a lot, and while what she did is fucked up, I choose to believe she had a good reason."

My eyes well with the tears I'm no longer able to stop, and I struggle to take in air. "But you haven't asked her? I'm confused.

So, according to your parents, you have a girlfriend?" *This can't be happening again.*

"Yes, I have a girlfriend. *You!* You're my girlfriend. There's no one else. This is just a... Fuck! I don't even know how to explain it properly without telling you things I was told in confidence over the years."

"I need something, Nate. *Anything.* Because right now, I feel like I'm the other woman, and I won't put up with that again."

Anger rises in him, and he looks positively murderous. "Again? What the fuck happened in the past? Who—"

I shoot him a glare because he can't seriously be concerned about my past relationships right now when he's hurting me right now.

He cringes at my look, and his shoulders drop. "I'm sorry, it's just that the thought of anyone hurting you absolutely kills me."

"You're hurting me, Nate."

His eyes flash to mine as pain radiates from his entire body. My heart clenches until I realize it shouldn't. This is all on him.

"I'm going to meet with my parents and Liv before the game tomorrow to get to the bottom of this. But, for now, I can't just throw her to the wolves." *Okay, but what about me?*

I stare at him for a moment, unsure what to say, unsure what he wants me to say, until an idea comes to mind. "Have you thought that maybe she wants you back? Do you want her back?"

"No! To both. She has a few things going on that sometimes lead her to make poor decisions, but that's it. I promise I'll fix this."

"Okay, I understand. To a degree, but the one thing that makes little sense... If your parents think you're back with your ex, what do they think happened to me? Or was I never in the picture?" I say, raising an eyebrow as I watch closely for his reaction. His flinch tells me everything I need to know. Standing up, I move to the door. I need to leave.

"Wait, please. We need to talk about this."

"I don't think there is anything you could say that—"

"*Fuck!*" He curses under his breath and grabs my hand. "I owe her, Cory. I owe her my life," he whispers, so it's harder to hear the pain in his voice.

"What does that mean?" I ask in concern.

Nate takes a deep breath and then sits, pulling me down beside him. I shake him off and stand up again before sending him an impatient glare. My arms cross.

"It means when I was young, and reckless, I drove Liv home from a party and crashed my truck. I wasn't drunk, but I wasn't sober either. It knocked me out on impact, while Liv had a broken arm and a cut forehead. Rather than focusing on her own injuries, she gently slid me along the bench seat to the passenger side and ran to get help.

"She told them she was driving, that she swerved to avoid hitting a deer. No one else was hurt. I just lost control because I was in a mood and being stupid. But I could have killed her. And she saved me. Not to mention the fact that I would have lost my scholarship and my place on the team if I were arrested."

I sit back down on the bed, and Nate sighs in relief. "I just need to talk to her tomorrow and sort this out *before* going to my parents. Maybe it's a misunderstanding."

"And what happens then? Are you going to tell them you have an actual girlfriend?"

"You're not a secret, Cory. I just don't talk to them about my love life."

I sigh. This is too much for me to process right now. This shit doesn't happen in real life. I should leave. I should end things right now and walk away with my head held high, but I can't. "Do you see her often?" I ask instead, obviously wanting to torture myself.

Nate shakes his head. "No. Only when I go home. And only once since we broke up."

"Do you *talk* often?" I know she called one time, but is that a regular thing?

He cringes, and my heart drops. *Shit!* That's another stab in the chest.

"So your parents and ex, or *fake* girlfriend, are going to your game tomorrow. If we're together, where does that leave me?"

"If?" he asks with a crestfallen expression.

"Just answer the question, Nate."

He peers up at me, looking so broken that I almost try to comfort him, but I keep still. "I've asked Dylan if he can get you some seats. He still has some allocation—"

"You know what? Don't worry about the tickets. *If* we're still together, I'll catch the next game." And with that, I leave. I know it's petty to storm out, but I just don't think my heart can take much more tonight.

"Cory—"

I don't stay to hear what he has to say. I need time. I'm dialing Summer's number before my feet even hit the top step, but for some reason, when she answers, I make a split second decision to lie. I generally tell her everything, but need to keep this to myself. At least, until I process exactly what happened.

Chapter Eight

Nate

As soon as I walk into the cafe the next morning, Liv's smile drops. She's not facing me directly, but I know she's seen the scowl on my face as I march toward her, ready for action. I don't want to be here. I'd rather be on Cory's doorstep, begging her to work this out. But the only way that's going to happen is if I fix this first.

"Nate, you're here," my mom says, standing from the table and pulling me into a hug. My scowl morphs into a smile as I greet my parents and sit down. "You're looking good. I must admit, I've worried no one's feeding you at that crazy house," she says, without her even waiting for me to say hello properly.

"We may not have staff, but we all eat," I say and laugh as though I'm joking. Dad laughs along with me, and I know it's because he knows I'm not. My dad was born with money, so despite being quite straight-laced now, he rebelled when he was a teen and declared he would never let money control him. To his credit, he's the most laid back senator I've ever seen. I don't even think it bothers him that I'm not following in his footsteps.

My mother, on the other hand, married into money, so some might say she's still enjoying the life it brings. It's safe to say she doesn't understand why anyone would voluntarily live without it.

Dad offers me his hand, and I shake it, making sure I apply the correct amount of pressure. Handshakes are a big deal in his line of work. So we've both come to perfect them. "Are you ready for the game today, son?"

"Almost," I say honestly, giving Liv a bit of a side eye. "Food would definitely help get me across the line." I smile as I pick up the menu. "What's everyone having? Liv and I will go order."

We collect the orders and head to the counter. As soon as we're out of earshot, I let her have it. "What's going on? Why are you here, and why are you telling my parents we're back together? You know I have a girlfriend. Is this some kind of joke? Because if it is, it's not fucking funny."

"Shhh! Can you keep your voice down? I'll explain everything if you just chill the fuck out."

I glare at her but do as she says because, for one, I want her to explain, and two, the woman in line in front of us is giving me strange looks.

"Explain away," I whisper.

I genuinely listen to her every word, and by the time we sit back down at the table, she's filled me in. It may be a fucked up story, but it wasn't a long one. In short, she's in a bind, and while I told her I don't want to be a part of her lies, I said I'd wait until she wasn't away with my parents before I tell them the truth. I'm not a complete asshole.

The rest of lunch is pleasant, and I'm just about to say my good-byes when Mom chooses that moment to throw us a curveball I wasn't expecting. "Now that you're back together, presumably for the long hall this time, I'd like to talk to you both about making things a little more public. It would really help your dad if we could talk about some exciting family news."

I spit out my drink as my eyes flash to Dad's. He shrugs his shoulders and looks down at his phone, not wanting anything to do with this request. *What is she even asking me?*

If me being in a relationship helped Dad's cause, I'm more than happy to talk about Cory, but this mess with Liv is another story.

My teammate, Luke, arrives at that moment to give me a lift to the game and I've never been so happy to see him. "I have to leave for pre-game training, Mom. But how about I call you this week to discuss it."

She smiles up me as she reaches across the table and squeezes my hand. "Thank you, Nate. You know this means the world to us. I'm so happy the two of you have worked things out."

My lips pull into a thin line, and I nod. Right now, that's the best I can do.

I say my goodbyes and walk out the door. Liv follows under the guise of wanting some alone time before I leave. "I'm sorry, Nate. I really am, but I need this. Is there any way I can change your mind?" She grabs my bicep with a panicked look.

"I'm sorry, Liv. I really am."

She sighs and pulls me into a hug. "Let me know if you change your mind."

I reluctantly hug her back, aware of Luke watching on. Before this, we were still good friends. I need to remember that. This isn't entirely her fault, and I don't want to ruin our friendship. I'm not changing my mind, of that I'm sure, but I could at least be nice about it.

Luke raises his eyebrows as Liv walks away. "Who's the hottie?"

I roll my eyes and push him in the direction of his car. "Family friend; now, let's go," I say, hoping he'll drop it, and, lucky for me, he does. The last thing I need is for him to be chatting my head off about Liv when all I want to do is think about Cory and how desperate I am to see her. I want to call her, but with Luke in the car I'll have to wait until after the game.

* * *

The water pours over my shoulders as I stare at the floor, listening to my teammates excited cheers. We've just won our first game of the season. Spirits are high. The guys are singing and dancing and already predicting championships. As soon as I'm out of the shower, they'll expect me to join in. And I will. Of course, I will. On the outside, everything is fine. If I hadn't played so shit, everyone would be none the wiser. Inside, I'm a mess. This morning's shitshow aside, my mind is still stuck in my bedroom, watching Cory walk away.

When she left last night, I was absolutely devastated. I shouldn't have been surprised at her reaction, but I didn't think she'd leave before we'd worked things out. It's completely fucking with my head.

I turn the shower off when I've hit the limit of appropriate time, wanting to avoid getting questions. As soon as the last drop falls, I flip the switch on happy-go-lucky Nate and throw myself head first into the madness.

When it becomes apparent that I'm not going to be reamed out by the coaches, I can at least relax about one side of my life. I honestly expected the worst but didn't have enough brain space to care, so I just waited out the inevitable. Or not so inevitable as it may be.

I'm sure it helps that Dylan looks like absolute shit and is clearly going through something himself. Any teammates or coaches that would normally take notice seem to be focused on him. In fact, even I find myself wanting to focus on Dylan's issue. Anything to get myself out of my head.

The locker room starts to clear out, bringing me closer to the moment I'd been so looking forward to. All week I'd been picturing Cory waiting for me after the game. But that wasn't going to be happening. She wasn't even here.

Confronting Liv today had been rough. I didn't want to hurt her, but at the same time, Cory is my number one priority. As I think back to her reasons, I cringe. Why does life have to be so damn complicated?

I'm ripped out of my thoughts when a towel hits me in the face. "Snap out of it, Edwards," our captain says with another towel locked and loaded, ready to throw. "You had a bad game; we all get them. Make sure you excel in the next one."

If I can sort this shit out, I know the next game will be fine. I just have to get through the post-game celebrations, and then I can talk to Cory tomorrow.

○ ○ ○

I'm officially over the party a few hours in. I'd tossed Dylan my room keys a little while ago, so I can't even hide out there. Though, if I had my time over, I'd still give them to him. He's definitely going through something, and after seeing him with his ex, I knew he needed the break more than I did.

When I'm finally ready to call it a night, I check on Dylan before I decide how to sneak away. I find him looking even worse than before, completely uninterested in my company, but an idea comes to mind.

Finding a quiet spot, I call Summer, praying that she's awake. She answers on the third ring, and I sigh in relief until she speaks. "Why didn't Cory go to your game? Are you the reason she's cleaning the apartment?"

Shit! Not even a hello. I should be thankful that Cory obviously hasn't told her what happened, but I'm more concerned about the fact that Cory needs someone right now, and after ten missed calls and an uncountable number of messages, I've realized that someone isn't me.

I clear my throat, ignoring Summer's questions. I need to work things out with Cory, without Summer's wrath. "I'm actually calling about Dylan."

"Dylan?" Her voice rises in intrigue. I'm telling you, those two need to get their shit sorted.

"Yeah. Something's going on with him, and he could use a friend."

She scoffs, and the phone crackles, like she's moving around the room, holding the phone with one hand.

"You're a friend," she states plainly, not making this easy on me. She's not wrong either. Maybe saying he needed a friend was too general.

"He needs you, Summer. *You.*" I could tell just looking at him he needed her. I don't know how, but I knew.

She's silent for a moment and then sighs. "Ugh! Okay, of course, I'll go. But you need to come here and fix whatever you did."

"I'm already on my way," I say as I walk to my car, determined to get Cory to hear me out.

Chapter Nine
Nate

C ory doesn't answer when I first knock on the door. In fact, it takes a solid five minutes of knocking before I hear movement. If I wasn't one hundred percent certain she was home, I'd have given up already.

She opens the door in her silk pajamas and a robe. Her hair is a mess, her cheeks are flushed from sleep, and her eyes are slightly red. My heart jumps at the sight of her.

"God. You're beautiful." I say, because it's exactly what I'm thinking. She's the most beautiful person I know, inside and out, and I hurt her.

Her eyelashes flicker a little as a slight blush appears, but the sadness doesn't leave her face. "It's almost midnight, Nate. Can we talk later? In the morning, maybe?"

"Absolutely not," I say, shocking us both with my sternness. She raises an eyebrow as though she's about to protest, so I pick her up and move her out of the doorway, before stepping inside.

"Nate…"

"No!" I snap. *I need to calm the fuck down.* I take a deep breath before continuing in a much softer tone. "We are fixing this, right now, because today sucked. I love football. I love hanging with the boys after a good win. I love it all. But today *sucked*. All I wanted to do was come to you."

"Why didn't you?" Cory asks, her voice holding its own austerity.

"It's actually not that easy to sneak away after a win. Just ask Dylan. He looked miserable for some reason, but he stayed."

Some annoyance melts from Cory's face, quickly replaced with concern. And while it stings that it takes mentioning someone else to soften her, I still love the part of her that cares so much.

"What happened to Dylan?" she asks quietly. Like she knows that's not the key issue right now.

"I wish I knew." I shrug. "But don't worry; I sent him the best person to help."

Cory eyes me in question.

"Summer." I wink and watch as a beautiful smile spreads across Cory's face. *Thank God.*

I take advantage of her better mood and bring the subject back to us, praying that I don't lose her again. "I'm so sorry, Cory. I can't stand you being upset with me."

"I have a good reason."

"I know you do. It's fucked up. But I'm sorting it out."

She pulls her lips into her mouth as though she wants to say something but is holding back. I draw my eyes to the movement, and I have to bite my own lips to stop myself from kissing her.

Cory's eyes drop to my mouth, and I can see the want in them. My heart beats a little faster. *We're not over.* She's still in this with me. I'm about to speak when Cory jumps in before me.

"It's infuriating, Nate. I only recently found out you were still friends with your ex, and now she's here, hanging out with your parents and telling them you're together. I don't want to be a part of this bullshit situation. Ugh! There shouldn't even *be* a situation. This is insane. I can't deal with this right now. I'm going back to bed. You can see yourself out."

I leap forward and grab her hand, pulling her back into me. Her body crashes into mine, and before she protests, I slam my lips into hers in a desperate kiss. I will not lose this girl, not now that I finally have her.

Cory's still at first, but when I curl my fingers under her jaw and raise it to deepen the kiss, she moans into my mouth, surrendering to me. *Fuck, yes!*

I grip her legs, lifting her until she wraps them around my waist. As soon as she's secured, I walk her backwards and push her against the wall, grinding into her. I know this solves nothing, but I need her close. Need to feel a connection with her. Need to know she still feels the same.

She moans again when our tongues clash, and it's almost my undoing. *Almost.*

"You should be leaving," Cory pants between kisses as she grips my hair, pulling me closer, completely contradicting her words.

With one hand holding her up, I curl the other around her wrist and raise it above her head. The movement causes her chest to rise closer to my face. Begging me to taste her.

She whimpers when I break the kiss, but it quickly turns into a cry of pleasure when I bite down on her nipple. "Still want me to go?" I tease.

Her head falls back against the wall as she moves her hips against me, seeking friction. I grind up into her and take her silence as the answer to my question, securing her in my arms and moving us to the couch.

Within seconds, our clothes come off, protections in place, and I'm sinking into her, groaning at the way her body molds to mine. Cory wraps her legs around me to pull me even closer as I grip the couch above her head, pounding into her as hard as I'll allow.

She meets me thrust for thrust, crying out when I change angles and bury myself deeper, hitting that spot that's difficult to find. Her nails dig into my back like she's intentionally causing pain, and I welcome the feeling.

Our sex life has been amazing lately. I have no complaints. But this is something else. It's hard and fast and primal, and... *shit!* Forcing myself to slow it down, I swivel my hips in a rhythmic motion to change the pace. Losing control is not an option.

When I feel her getting close, I move a hand between us, giving her the pressure she needs while biting her nipple once more.

She screams out in ecstasy, and squeezes me so tight I see stars as my release is ripped out of me. "*Fuck!*"

As soon as we're done, Cory stands and gets dressed. I follow her lead, and when I'm back in my clothes, I sit on the couch. *I'm still not leaving.*

"I know you're angry. I could feel it with every thrust. I fucked up. I know that. You have every right to be angry. But we're not breaking up. It's almost sorted anyway," I tell her, refusing to even entertain the idea of being without her. She may have every reason to walk away, but I know she doesn't want that.

"Almost?" she asks sceptically.

"Yes. I told her I don't want to be a part of her scheming. As soon as she's away from my parents, I'm telling them. I just didn't think it was fair to do it before their flight home together."

Cory's face softens again. "Okay. Out of curiosity, why did she do it?"

I sigh. I don't like to share other people's secrets, but I don't want to keep anything from Cory. "Liv's father died when she was little, and her mother was pretty messed up afterwards. She apparently disgraced the family and then disappeared. Our parents were best friends, and our families, well, we all come from money. I shouldn't be telling you all this, but I need you to trust me. To know...

"Her grandparents took her in, but they never treated her well, at least, not until we started dating. I guess being associated with our family helped them rise back up in the ranks. From the moment we got together, her grandparents changed. They started supporting her, both financially and emotionally. They helped her get a job at a great company and even seemed proud to be raising her. They weren't thrilled when we broke up, but what could they do?"

"Nothing," she answers.

"Not exactly." I pause, and Cory raises an eyebrow.

"Apparently, they added a condition to her trust fund. She needs to be in a relationship *with me*, or the money gets donated. They've got more money than anyone would ever want, but they need the power back and claim that they get that by associating with us... Anyway, like I said, it's bullshit."

Cory stares at me for a while. She knows my family is well off, but I never really talk about the politics that go along with it. She sighs and then frowns. "Does Liv have money without it?"

"She can work for it, like the rest of us." I say and watch as Cory raises her eyebrows in disbelief.

"Says the trust fund baby." *Ouch, that hurt. Is that what she thinks of me?*

My face scrunches as I think of a response.

"I'm kidding, Nate. But, it's not really fair for you to say that about her when it's something you'll never have to consider."

She has a good point, but it's out of my hands.

"When does the trust come in?"

"It doesn't matter."

"*When.*" Cory raises her voice slightly, confusing me. I thought I'd made the right decision, but she still seems mad.

I grip my shoulder and sigh. "In about a month. When she turns twenty-one."

"Okay," Cory says, nodding her head. *Huh?*

"Okay, what?"

"She can have a month, but I can't be with you. The thought of being intimate while you're still with her, it's just..." She trails off and shudders at whatever thought she has in mind.

"I'm not—" *with her... I* start to argue, but she cuts me off, and I cringe at the lack of emotion in her voice.

"Even if it's fake."

"Nope, I'm not interested. I'm telling my parents."

"It's just a month." *What the fuck? Am I in an alternate reality?*

"Cory, we are not breaking up over this."

"It's just a break."

"I don't give a fuck how you word it. This is crazy."

"Nate, what if she needs that money for something important?"

"She doesn't." *Is this really happening?*

She looks at me with pleading eyes, and I break. "Please." *God, why is she such a good person all the time?*

Fuck! I drop to the couch and rub my hands down my face. *What the fuck do I do?* I feel Cory sit beside me, but she remains silent.

"Okay." I say, meeting her gaze. "But we're not breaking up."

"Nate, I can't. I can't be the other woman," she says with a somber look on her face.

"You're not! This is your choice. Why would you even think that way?"

A tear escapes her eye, and I quickly brush it from her cheek before turning away and shaking my head. This is fucked up. So fucked up. I'm doomed if I do, doomed if I don't.

"Nate," Cory whispers, breaking into my thoughts. I nod in acknowledgment, but don't look up. "Nate, please. Look at me."

Her voice cracks, bringing my eyes straight to hers. She's staring back at me with more unshed tears and a pained expression.

"What aren't you telling me?" I ask, because none of this makes sense.

She sighs, suddenly finding one of her nails very interesting. "When my mom first had cancer, we almost went broke. It wasn't a great time for us, but we're lucky enough to have gotten through it. We don't know what's going on with Liv now or what might happen in the future. I couldn't live with myself knowing I could have helped and didn't."

God, this woman. I love her mom. She's as wonderful and kind as Cory. We've talked about her cancer before, but never about the financial implications.

"Plus, we both owe her. For saving your life." She smiles, but I still can't bring myself to return it.

"This is bullshit. You know that, right?"

"I do."

"I can't do this if we're broken up. I won't."

"It will be a bre—"

"Same thing. We have to stay together. If that means we can't be intimate, that's fine. But we're not breaking up."

There's silence for a moment, and then Cory finally speaks. "Okay," she whispers, and I sigh.

"Okay?"

"Yes. But, it's to keep up appearances only. I love you. I want to be with you. I won't tell a soul about her, and I expect you to do the same. I just can't..."

Fuck! That's less than ideal, but I get it, and I'll respect her wishes. I also suspect there's more to the story, but I know Cory's likely to brush me off if I ask. All I can do is accept this as is and talk to Liv to see if there's another way around it. The thought of not touching Cory pains me.

I nod and then pull her into a hug. "I'm going to fix this," I say for the millionth time, and I mean every word. "Then I'm going to spend my life making it up to you. I promise."

"This is not all on you. We'll get through it. But, for now, you should go." *What?*

She looks at me with a serious yet sympathetic expression. *Oh, right, sleeping over would be considered intimate. Fuck!* Leaving is the last thing I want to do, but I do as she asked.

I stand up and step between her legs before pressing my lips to her forehead. "I love you, Little Bit. I'm so sorry."

She sniffs and wipes her eyes, not even trying to hold back her tears anymore. When she meets my gaze, I break. I don't deserve her. The beautiful, intelligent, loving and kind woman sitting in front of me deserves the world, and instead, she gets my mess.

When she doesn't respond, I move to leave.

"I love you, too," she rasps as I reach for the door handle, and I sag in relief.

"I'll call you tomorrow. Well, today." I shrug and smile.

She nods but doesn't meet my eyes.

As soon as I'm in my truck, I scream out and curse myself for the mess I've made before driving home to drown my sorrows in alcohol.

Chapter Ten

Cory

I should have known that keeping up appearances wouldn't be easy. I had planned to spend the month focused on studying. To catch up on the work and reading I'd been neglecting since Nate and I got together. But, no. Of course, Summer and Dylan would become best friends that spend every waking second together at the same time Nate and I need to spend time apart.

"Cory!" one of the guys yells from across the bar as soon as Summer and I step inside. Because, yep, she somehow convinced me to go to a bar with them. I take a deep breath and put on a smile. *I can do this. Just act normal.*

When we approach the table, the guys clear a spot for Summer but nothing for me. I internally cringe as I realize why. I *always* perch on Nate's lap. Trying not to make a big deal out of it, I sit down and give him a quick smile and hello. His hands wrap around my waist, pulling me closer, and I flinch.

Nate sighs and releases his hold ever so slightly. Enough that he's barely touching me, but it still looks like he is. *God, this is going to be a long month.*

"Nate was just saying that you missed our killer game on the weekend," his teammate, Luke says, waggling his finger at me with a tsk tsk.

My eyes flash to Nate's as I wonder what exactly he said. He gives me the faintest head shake, as if to say nothing else was said, so I turn back to Luke with a grin. "Did he also mention that I had a family engagement party?" A lie. "And that I secretly watched the game on my phone." Not a lie. Well, the phone part is. I watched it on my laptop.

Nate curses quietly behind me, and I regret my words. I didn't say them to make him feel bad. I move my hand to squeeze his leg but think better of it. If I expect him to keep his hands to himself, I have to do the same.

The conversation moves on to other topics as our group all come and go between the bar and the dance floor. Dylan and Summer talk like they've been best friends for years, and I smile at their happiness.

I'm just convincing myself that the next month won't be so bad when Luke opens his big mouth again. "Not dancing tonight, Cory? You and Nate are always on the dance floor." *Shit!*

I should have prepared myself for this. "You're right, Luke, but—"

"I told her I wasn't feeling it tonight. I felt a twitch during training today and don't want to make it worse," Nate offers, saving me from coming up with an explanation.

"Fuck! I hope that's a joke, Edwards. We need you out there."

"I had it checked. Nothing to worry about. Just have to take it easy today. We'll be back out there before you know it," he says, waving his hand toward the dancers.

"I guess that explains why you're a bit off tonight, too, Nate," Dylan adds, and I flinch. "Make sure you keep on top of it."

Maybe keeping up appearances is going to be a lot harder than I thought.

The next few weeks are hard. *Really hard.* All I've wanted to do, for every second of every day, is to be with Nate. Just hold his hand, or hug him... with meaning. When we're around friends, I continue to keep up the facade. But to be honest, the time around friends is becoming few and far between. I can't stand the lies, or seeing the tortured look on Nate's face. A look I know is reflected on mine. The whole thing just about kills me.

Technically, I'm the one who got us into this situation, so I could easily get us out of it, but I just want everything to be sorted before we're truly *us* again. I need it for my own peace of mind. *Am I asking too much?*

Tonight, we're supposed to be having dinner with Dylan and Summer. I tried to get out of it, but Summer put her foot down. Saying they'd barely seen us. They organized it for seven pm. Nate arrived on time, but Dylan and Summer are MIA. If I didn't think we were doing such a good job at hiding our issues, I'd think they had planned this. But they're probably out somewhere, enjoying each other's company, pretending they don't want more than just friendship and have forgotten the time. *Do I sound bitter? Oops.*

Being alone with Nate feels different from how it used to be. There's a tense energy surrounding us that's impossible to miss, and our once comfortable silences now feel anything but.

Nate runs his hand down his face before starting to speak, but I shake my head. "Please don't apologize. Let's just enjoy our time together and try to forget the crap that's going on," I say, because focusing on our situation, on Liv, is the last thing I want to do.

Nate raises an eyebrow and smirks.

"I don't mean completely forget," I laugh. "I just mean, let's not talk about it."

Nate rolls his eyes jokingly and smiles. His playful expression helps ease the tension a little as we stand on opposite sides of the counter and talk. With Nate's football and the fall semester starting, we've both been busy, so avoiding alone time has been easy. It's only now as we casually chat about everyday mundane stuff I realize how much I miss the friend that he'd become, as well as the boyfriend.

We've just branched off into deeper conversation when Summer calls. My brows furrow in confusion as I put the call on speaker. I haven't even said hello when she speaks.

"Cory, hi. I'm so sorry. I know you were expecting us, but we were halfway home when I realized my phone was missing. Turns out, I left it at the bar. Lucky, Joel remembered me putting it down. Anyway, we went past that theater I love, and... Oh! Did you know Dylan's *never* seen The Wizard of Oz? Crazy, right? It's playing here in twenty minutes, so Joel and I told Dylan he had to watch it. If that's okay? I'm sure you're enjoying your alone time with Nate, but I wanted to ask..."

I huff out a frustrated laugh at her rant, because how could I have possibly known that. And I can't even be annoyed because she doesn't know what's going on.

Before I can respond that it's fine, she giggles uncontrollably. *Is she drunk?* Well, she did mention a bar.

"Have you been drinking?" I ask, standing up and walking towards the kitchen to pour a glass of water. I pause and look at the liquid in my hand, realizing my natural instincts to take care of Summer are in full force, even though she's not here.

Summer's silent for a minute before drawing out a long, "Maaybee," and then giggling.

That's a yes, then.

There's a slight commotion on the line, and Dylan's voice comes through, "Come on, little one; let's get you some water. Sorry, Cory."

I sigh with relief and smile. She has someone else looking out for her. *Maybe I don't have to worry?*

"I thought Cory was the little one?" Nate calls out as he heads toward the kitchen, shooting a wink my way.

"Actually, I've heard that's you, Nate," Summer teases just before the call disconnects.

My head flies back, almost hitting the cabinet behind me, and I laugh so hard. More than I have in a while.

Nate stares at me with a fake, hurt expression. "Easy there. It's not that funny," he says as a small smirk forms on his lips.

"Come on; it's pretty funny," I say between laughs, trying, unsuccessfully, to control myself. I'm not even sure it is *that* funny. It's certainly not true. Just one of those moments when I laugh for no reason.

A huge smile breaks out on Nate's face, even though I'm laughing at his expense.

He watches me until I finally calm down and then steps forward, running his thumb across my cheek. It's so light and quick that if my eyes were closed, I may have thought I Imagined it. I shiver and immediately tense up. *God, I wish we weren't in this mess.*

"Hearing your laugh, with all that we have going on, means *everything* to me. You have a beautiful laugh and smile, and I'm so sorry I've taken that away from you lately."

I swallow a lump in my throat. This is just as much my fault as his. "I'm sorry, too. I know you probably think I'm doing this to punish you, even though it was my idea, but I'm not. I just—"

"I get it Cory. Mostly. You don't need to explain it right now. But one day, I hope you do."

He's right. I probably wouldn't be acting this way if my previous relationships hadn't screwed me over so badly. That fact that he's being so understanding about it should speak volumes. *So, why can't I tell him?*

I sigh as Nate stares at my hand on my face. I hadn't even realized I'd been tracing the pattern he'd just made with his thumb. I pull my hand away quickly and tuck it behind my back.

Nate sighs and looks off into space. We're both quiet for a moment until he turns back to me with a tentative smile. "I have an idea, but you're going to have to keep an open mind?" he says with hesitation.

Huh? My eyebrows pull together and my lips purse. "Nate, I don't think—"

"Please, just hear me out. I'd like us to try something." he says, biting back a nervous smile, and I know he's up to something.

"I'll need the details before I agree." I try to keep a straight face, but I'm sure he can tell I'm intrigued.

"Wouldn't expect anything else," he says with a wink. "I want us to talk without senses."

My eyes widen with shock and confusion. "Ah... What?"

"Well, not *no* senses. That's unrealistic, but minimal senses. No touch, no sight, no taste..." He bounces his eyebrow at the last one, and I shiver at the thought of him touching me again. "Only sound and smell are allowed. And I'm only allowing smell because it's difficult to control. It's not like I'm going to make you block your nose."

I laugh because he's crazy and I don't really know another appropriate reaction. He must take my laugh as confusion because he continues trying to convince me.

"I want us to talk, and really listen to each other, and to feel the energy in the room. Maybe that sounds corny, but I need more time with you. And if eliminating the pressure helps, then I'll do anything."

My hand reaches out to gives his a quick squeeze without my permission. "I happen to love corny," I say, because it's true.

Nate smiles widely knowing he's got me. "Great, I'll be right back."

My heart jumps as I realize what he's saying. "Wait? You want to do this now?" I call after him as he walks towards my room.

"Now's a great time. You heard Summer; she won't be home for hours. But I'll message Dylan just in case." he says, pulling his phone from his packet.

I shake my head and frown. *What did I just agree to?*

Chapter Eleven

Nate

"This is silly. Why did I agree to this?" Cory complains as she ties her makeshift blindfold. I wave my hand in her face, finding no reaction, and then secure my own. God, this feels weird. I'm actually wondering why I suggested it myself. No, I suggested it to give us a chance to talk, really talk, and listen. No distractions.

Before Summer called, we were finding our way back into our groove, but it wasn't enough. We never really ventured outside of the easy everyday topics, and I had a feeling that Cory was about to call it a night. I wanted the chance to talk without fear. Without seeing the other person as we bear our souls.

Our conversation starts off back on the safer topics before finally moving into deeper territory. We've been talking for a while when Cory asks something that's obviously been on her mind.

"Why did you and Liv break up?"

I don't answer right away, taking time to think about how best to approach this. My face scrunches, and I grip my shoulder. "Ah..." I pause before deciding to throw it all out there.

"We started drifting from the moment I jumped in my box-filled truck and headed for college. She never wanted to go to college and couldn't understand why I'd move away when there was one close to home. She knew I had the scholarship, she got that, but considering my family has money, and I don't want a career in the NFL, I think she took it to mean I was moving away on purpose. Which isn't *exactly* true, but it's also *not* wrong.

"I had to get out of that town. People only ever saw me as the son of Nathan James Edwards, the senator, and always expected me to get into politics. Don't get me wrong, I love my family, and my dad's great at what he does, but it's not for me. I'm content with getting my teaching degree and molding the minds of the future generations. Actually, that's not fair. I'm not content. I'm excited."

Cory laughs at that. She's heard me talk about teaching many times before.

"Anyway, I left on purpose, but it wasn't to get away from Liv. In the early days, I flew home a lot to see her, but then things got busy, and I'd find that when I went home, my mind remained here, on the new life I was building. Liv started hanging out with new people and called less and less until we eventually decided we'd be better off as friends."

"You both decided?" Cory says as she shifts in her seat.

Now's the moment. I can tell her the truth. Or lie by omission. Since I want this girl in my life forever, I decide on the truth. "Yes, it was mutual... in the beginning. But six months into our breakup, she said she wanted me back. At that point, I already had my eye on someone else. Someone I couldn't get out of my head. Someone I still can't get out of my head."

Cory takes in a sharp breath, but is otherwise silent. "I first saw you when you were walking around campus with Summer and an older couple, who I now know are your mom and dad. I'm guessing you were checking out the campus or getting your bearings. You looked so excited with your map and notebook. Something about you just struck me, and I was desperate to see you again.

"I didn't know if you'd actually enrolled, but when classes started the next semester, I looked for you. A lot. I looked until I'd convinced myself you weren't here. And then... well, you know this part. An adorable little freshman showed up in my public speaking class, and the rest is history."

"Wow! Okay. So you tried to stalk me?" I can hear the smile in her voice, and it brings a smirk to my lips.

"I tried, but since I never found you, I obviously wasn't good at it."

I hope Cory concentrates on the positive of that story and not the fact that, one, Liv wanted me back, and two, that I liked *her* for so long and never approached her. The reason for the latter is still something I'm trying to deal with.

Cory shifts, causing the arm of the couch to creak. "And... You don't think Liv still wants you now?" *Shit!*

"No, I don't. She was pretty forward about it last time. This is different." I honestly don't think that's why Liv's doing it, it's not like we're spending any time together during this lie.

"Or she's changed tact." Cory mumbles, and I flinch. Is she worried?

"I don't—"

"Never mind, enough about her."

I frown. She's so far away and I want to reassure her... Even though I can't touch her, I still want her close. Especially now

"Are you going to sit that far away all night? I'm not allowed to touch you, so you have nothing to worry about," I coax, hoping she shuffles closer.

"How about we play a game?" she says, changing the subject. "A question game, like we've played before, but different. Every time you get a correct answer, you can move closer to me." Her voice is full of sass now. Like she's completely moved on, though I know she hasn't. I welcome the change of topic.

"Done! What's the game?"

"We each ask a question about ourselves. If you answer correctly, you can move closer. If I answer correctly, I'll move away." *What!?* Cory laughs as though she can sense my puzzled expression. "Every game needs to be challenging," she says and shuffles in her seat. I'm imagining her moving to sit on her knees, knowing it's her go-to position when she's interested in something.

"Okay, I'll start," I say, trying to think of something she'll never be able to answer. "How many touchdowns have I made in my college football career?"

"Come on," she laughs. "You need to try harder than that... three."

Two were in my first year. I didn't think she'd get that, considering she was still a sophomore in high school.

"I can't move back any further. You'll have to answer two correctly before you can move forward."

I roll my hand to signal for her to ask me, then remember we've *both* lost our sight. Not just me. Clearing my throat, I say, "Ask away."

"Have I ever dyed my hair?"

"No," I answer quickly. That's an easy one.

"Okay, I gave you that one. When did Summer and I last fight?"

Damn. Those two are close as close can be. Even when Cory started spending more time with me and Summer distanced herself, I could still see the love they had for each other. This is tricky. It's a complete guess. "After she moved in with you in high school?"

Summer had a falling out with her family, no one knows why, but she moved in with Cory and her family when she was sixteen. Cory huffs out a laugh. Guess that means I'm wrong.

"Good try, but we fight more often than that. We had a huge blow-up last year when she started staying out all night. I got worried when she didn't call, and we fought about the fact that I was treating her like a child."

I'm about to speak when Cory adds, "I won that fight, and to this day, she texts any night she's not coming home."

I laugh, hearing the smirk in her voice, and shake my head.

"Okay, my turn. I need some wins. What age did I lose my first tooth?"

"Ah, come on. Six?"

"Ha! Five. I'm moving closer."

This goes on for another thirty minutes. Every time I think I'm going to reach her, she throws out some ridiculous question, and I move a few inches away. It's safe to say that my forward movements are definitely bigger than my backward ones, but since she can't see me, she's never going to know. *Ha. I'm so smart, and twelve, apparently.*

Cory takes a deep breath, like she's preparing herself for something, and when she asks her next question, I'm completely thrown. "How many times have I pleasured myself since we started the no intimacy rule?" Her voice is breathy, changing the energy in the room in an instant.

Fuck!

My heart rate picks up as my shorts tighten. I wasn't even aware she'd *ever* done that. I mean, I know girls do, but we've talked about it, and the question has always embarrassed her. And, she's always said no. My gut says to answer none, that she's just teasing, but for some reason, I try another response. "Three," I squeak out, immediately clearing my throat. "Once a week. So, three," I say again and wait for her reply.

Cory doesn't say a word, but I feel the couch shift as she moves closer to me. *Fuck! I'm right.* My mind conjures up images of how that might look, and my shorts grow so tight it hurts.

"Sa... same question for you," I say, just above a whisper.

Cory intakes a sharp breath and then sighs. I've never been so desperate to see her. "Daily," she says, and I thank my lucky stars that she's wrong. I move closer, causing a buzz of energy to zap between us.

"How many then?" she asks, her voice quivering. She's definitely as affected by this as I am.

"Is that my question?" I ask, hopeful that it is so I can move even closer.

"Yes," she rasps, and I groan.

"None," I answer. "Not once. I've been punishing myself for putting us through this. I want the next hand, the *only* hand to touch me, to be yours."

Cory moans, sliding closer to me at the same moment I move to her. We both stop before we touch. We're so close, I can almost feel her nose brushing against mine as her breath warms my cheek. My whole body comes alive as I feel her beside me.

"Your turn," she whispers.

"If I could touch you anywhere on your body, right now, where would you want me to touch?" It's not a question about me, and technically breaks the rules of the game, but so did hers, so she better allow it.

I hear shuffling around, but have no idea what she's doing. My pulse quickens to a scary speed, and my hands clench beside my legs to stop myself from touching her. "Maybe here?" she whispers in a husky voice. I groan uncontrollably. *Oh, Hell. Is she touching herself?* "Or maybe here?" she continues, and my body shudders with need.

"You're killing me, Cory. Please, tell me what you're doing? Where is your hand?" My voice bleeds desperation. This isn't a want. I *need* to know the answer.

I feel more movement, and a slight brush of my knee before her breath tickles my ear. "I'd take you touching me anywhere right now, Nate. Anywhere. You. Like."

And just like that, all bets are off. I reach forward to touch her as my phone suddenly rings, causing us both to jump apart, breaking the spell we're under. I want to hurt someone. Specifically, the someone choosing *now* to call me. "*Fuck!*" I reach back blindly, pushing a few buttons until the noise stops. *Fuck, fuck!* Have I said that already?

When I suggested this, I never thought we'd end up here. I take a few deep breaths to calm myself until my breathing slows to a normal pace. When I'm finally able to focus on something other than Cory's voice, I remove the blind fold quietly, and my eyes instantly seek her out. She's staring back at me with a flushed and slightly embarrassed expression. It's so fucking cute, I have to sit on my hands so I don't reach over to her and finish what I think we were starting.

My phone rings a second time, then a third, so I finally check the screen. My best friend's name flashes in front of me. *He's a dead man.* Shane and I grew up together back home. He moved to attend the University of San Fran for a basketball scholarship when I moved here. We live close enough that we can still catch up, but far enough that we don't do it as much as we'd like. *Not that I ever want to see his face again after today.*

I show Cory the screen, and she smiles. Fucking smiles. Maybe I'm the only one sexually frustrated. Well, she is pleasuring hers. *Nope, don't think about that. Back to the call.* Cory and Shane have never met in person, but a friendship has grown between them over video calls. One that I'm now regretting.

"This better be good, asshole," I scold.

"Hey! What did I do?"

"Just tell me what you need."

He scoffs and is most likely rolling his eyes. Never one to put up with my crap. "Just calling to make sure you're coming to my birthday celebration next week." *Shit!*

"Ah…" Worst friend in the world, but I'd actually forgotten about it. This thing with Cory is taking up one hundred percent of my available brain space.

"Put Cory on the phone, Edwards," Shane says, without giving me a chance to say anything else. He's the only one who knows what's going on between us, and that's because I wanted someone to fill me in on what's being said within our family units. His parents are close to mine, too.

"You're already on speaker; say what you want to say." I roll my eyes as Cory smiles again.

He launches straight into his attack. "Cory, I know you and Nate are going through things, and the less time you spend together, the better. I get it; I really do." I brace myself for his but. "But, you need to get your sweet ass to the Firelight club on Saturday night or prepare for my wrath. I'm only going to turn twenty one once, and I have a feeling we're going to be in each other's lives for years to come. It's best if you don't start our friendship off on the wrong foot." He's joking, but I'm not sure Cory realizes that.

My eyes flick to hers, prepared for a little wrath right now, but to my shock, she's smiling. She's just about to answer him when he adds, "Plus, isn't there only two days left by then? Olivia turns twenty-one just after me. My brother's the only one who'll know Nate, and he couldn't care less about your business. Come; celebrate and let loose. You'll be practically free. You can even make it your first date," he jokes. *Asshole.*

"Fine," Cory states, sounding bored or annoyed with a huge smile on her face, as she holds back a laugh that Shane can't see.

"Thank you. I appreciate it, Cory, because the jerkface next to you didn't have to say it, but I know he wouldn't go without you."

Cory's eyes flash to mine in question. He's telling the truth, but I wasn't going to tell her that. She shakes her head but her smile remains. "We'll be there, Shane. Both of us."

"That's what I like to hear! Now, tell me, Nate. She was fucking with me, wasn't she? I bet she had a big smile on her face."

"Nope, she looks pretty angry," I tease.

"Shit! Sorry, Cory. I didn't—"

My lie is blown the second she giggles.

"I knew it. You both suck. I'll see you Saturday night. Hope you lose the game, Nate."

"Goodbye, Shane." He hangs up before I've finished speaking.

I turn to Cory with a smile. "He's right. We're practically free." I bounce my eyebrows suggestively.

"I'll give you Saturday. But until then, nothing. And no more alone time. I'm not going to lie and say I didn't enjoy this, but it was a slip. It won't happen again. We can last until Saturday."

I can do that. I've come this far; I can definitely last until Saturday. I'm excited just thinking about it. "Prepare to be blown away by my PDA."

Cory laughs, and I realize, more than anything, I just want to hold her, hear her tell me she loves me, and fall asleep with her in my arms. I mean, of course I'd also love a bit of whatever might have happened today, but that can wait.

My pulse quickens as I picture running my fingers through her hair and pressing a kiss to her forehead, just holding her. Saturday can't come quick enough.

Chapter Twelve

Cory

I jump up and down as Nate runs out onto the field after halftime. Ever since I decided that tonight we'd end our little physical strike, I've felt like a huge weight has been lifted from my shoulders. The walls I'd erected are scattered on the floor, and now I'm ready to get back to normal. Back to the Nate and Cory we once were.

I'm watching Nate's game with Summer and our friend Joel. It's the first time Summer's been to a game since the incident with her family, and to say I'm in awe of her strength would be a major understatement. She denies it, of course, but it must have taken a lot for her to come tonight and support her friends.

I watch Nate as he lines up for the next play and can't help but think about what I've missed in the last few weeks. I don't regret my decision to keep my distance. I was protecting my heart, but I still wish things could have been different. Although, in the scheme of things, it's only a short amount of time when your plan is forever.

The crowd goes wild, me included, when Dylan runs toward the end zone. Jumping to my feet, I scream his name but find myself scanning the field for Nate at the same time. I love being here. I love seeing my man in his element. It's time I forgot about everything going on and just enjoyed myself.

Nate's the first to walk out of the locker room after the game. He beelines for me with purpose, his eyes locked on mine and full of heat. "It's Saturday," he announces before slamming his lips to mine in a bruising kiss. A kiss that lasts all of five seconds before one of his teammates knocks shoulders with him, laughing on his way out.

Nate groans at the interruption as I smirk and walk off toward the exit. *We've got all night.*

I say a quick goodbye to Summer, then head to Nate's truck, just as desperate to get to this party as he is. Although, I'm trying not to show it.

The drive to the city is hell. You could cut the sexual tension with a knife. Nate sneaks glances at me regularly throughout the trip, as though he wants to say something, but he keeps quiet. I'm actually surprised he isn't pulling over to jump me right here in the car. I'm even more surprised to realize that I *want* him to do it, but to my annoyance, he drives on.

When we arrive, my heart rate increases at the thought of finally being free. As soon as Nate parks his truck, he's out and racing around to open my door. I smile at him in thanks as he takes my hand and helps me down. "I'm not letting go of this all night," he growls, then moves to shut the door.

Nate's true to his word, clasping my hand as we make our way around the room. We find Shane near the bar, and I finally meet the man face to face. He's even better looking than I remember, with messy brown hair and stunning blue-green eyes. He's wearing a dress shirt with the sleeves rolled up, drawing the attention of ninety percent of the girls nearby.

"Cory!" he yells as he engulfs me in a hug and rocks me from side to side. The motion almost causes me to drop Nate's hand, but he holds on tight.

"In the flesh," I say, smiling at his ability to instantly make me feel comfortable.

He releases me before giving Nate the same hug treatment, and I can't help but laugh. Nate has a huge smile on his face, looking more relaxed than he's been in weeks. Our time apart has definitely been hard on him. On both of us.

We chat with Shane for a bit until he's pulled into another conversation. We're about to head out to the beer garden when Nate's recognized by some football fans. I should be annoyed at the interruption, but I always get a buzz seeing so many people admiring my man.

"Are you going to make the playoffs this year?" one guy asks as the other watches on intently. I can sense this isn't going to be a brief conversation, so I excuse myself to use the bathroom. Nate reluctantly releases my hand for the first time, but I feel his eyes on me for my entire walk across the room.

A woman is cursing when I enter the ladies' room, and my automatic instinct is to go to her aid. "Goddammit. Jesus. Fuck my life. Of course, this would—" She pauses as soon as she sees me before dropping her head into her hands. "Ugh! I'm so sorry. Please ignore me."

Ignoring people that might need help is not really my strong suit, so I take a step closer and lean against the counter. "Are you okay?" I ask, taking in her appearance. I'd say she's a couple of years younger than me, maybe even a senior in high school. She looks like a kick-ass rebel with her short tartan skirt and knee-high combat boots. If she wasn't close to tears, I'd even tell her how awesomely badass she looks. But instead, I gently squeeze her arm in comfort.

She gazes at me through the mirror, like she's trying to figure out if I actually want an answer. I raise an eyebrow in question, eliciting a smile.

"Sorry; I'm okay. I just..." she trails off but raises her hand *and* hair up for me to see. I wince sympathetically when I see what brought on the very creative language.

The poor girl has managed to get her hair tangled in and around not one, but two, of her beautiful gold, expensive looking bracelets.

I rush around her until I'm closer to her hair. "Please let me help. This must hurt like crazy," I say, slowly reaching out for her hair.

Her eyes widen in shock before they narrow in suspicion. "Why are you being so nice to me?" she asks, like I'm helping her move house instead of simply untangling her hair.

I laugh at her clear disbelief as I continue to pull strand after strand free. "Why wouldn't I be nice to you?"

"I guess because the first two girls just left me here, and I assumed you'd do the same." *What the hell? Some people...*

Shaking my head, I gently continue with my task. We're both silent for a few minutes until the girl finally speaks. "Are you here for the twenty-first or just out partying?"

"The twenty-first. You?"

"Same! How do you know Shane?" She smiles excitedly, and it meets her eyes for the first time.

I'm just about to answer when a few drunk women blast through the door, check their make-up, and then dart back out again, without even taking a breath from their conversation. Or acknowledging our existence, for that matter. They move so quickly that we both stand, frozen, until the door clicks shut behind them. After a momentary pause, our eyes meet, and we burst out laughing.

The moment thaws the last remaining iciness between us, and from then on, we're laughing until she's finally freed from her hair hell. After saying goodbye, I realize we never discussed how we both know Shane. Maybe I could have gotten some juicy gossip about him.

When I walk out of the bathroom, I see Nate talking to a beautiful woman near the bar. She has dark brown hair that sits perfectly around her shoulders and a figure that would make swimwear models jealous. He's smiling at her, but anyone can see the tension in his expression.

I approach with caution, not wanting to interrupt their conversation, but as soon as Nate spots me, he reaches for my hand and links our fingers, easing my concern. I settle by his side, giving his fingers a squeeze at the exact moment he drops my hand and a random arm curls around my shoulder. *What?*

"Nate!" a voice sounds from across the room, but I can't see the owner. "Gah! I've missed you," the approaching voice gushes.

My eyes widen as I look at Nate in confusion. His face contorts with pain before he eyes me apologetically, his arm going around the dark haired beauty beside him as he watches the girl I now recognize as my bathroom buddy running up to meet us.

Before I can react, or even process this moment, I'm pulled slightly further away. Until then, I'd forgotten about the extra limb that had suddenly attached itself to me.

Looking up at the culprit, I find Shane's turquoise eyes staring back at me, full of sympathy. *What is going on?* He leans in to whisper in my ear as the bubbly girl arrives.

"Little Sis. What are you doing here?" Nate asks, almost seething.

Little Sis? Shit! Of course, his sister's here. We should have just waited two more days. I should have stayed at home. I take a step back, because I want no part of this, but Shane holds me in place.

His sister, Emily, I think her name is, looks around sheepishly. "I'm d—"

"Never mind. Shane?" Nate cuts her off, looking over in our direction. When his eyes lock on Shane, they narrow for a second before his features soften. I feel guilty, even though I've done nothing wrong, and pull out of Shane's strange hug. Shane grips my hand to stop me from moving again, and whispers a quick "please" under his breath.

Nate nods his head toward the back door before storming that way without looking back. The gorgeous girl he'd been talking to racing after him.

"Fuck, this isn't going to end well," Shane says as he pulls me in the same direction. Nate's sister stares at us in confusion but stays where she is.

As soon as we're in the hall, Nate turns to Shane, his eyes ablaze with anger. "Why the fuck would you not tell me you invited her? You even used the whole 'no one knows you, you'll be free' speech. Well, guess what? She fucking knows me. *Really* well."

Shane's expression turns to anger rather than guilt, suggesting he had nothing to do with it. "Which *her* are you referring to?" he asks, confusing me completely. "If you mean Emily, she's dating my brother. I only found out last night and told him not to bring her. But if you're referring to Liv, she wasn't on my invite list."
Liv?

The girl with Nate scoffs, but remains silent. My eyes snap to her as I suddenly realize who I'm standing beside. "Holy shit," I mumble under my breath. At least, I thought it was under my breath, but when three sets of eyes flash to mine, I second guess myself.

"Cory, I'm so sorry. I honestly didn't know..." That comes from Nate, quickly followed by a, "I would never put you through this, Cory. Please believe me," from Shane.

I think it's safe to say my suspicions are confirmed. The fourth person in our little group is none other than Nate's ex, Liv. *Tonight is going to suck.*

I'm just about to let everyone know that I'm going home when Emily walks through the door, arm in arm with a young boy who looks almost identical to Shane, but with longer hair. Shane grabs my hand and links our fingers, causing me to stiffen as Nate curses under his breath.

"Emily, James, thanks for coming. Sorry about before." He gives James a look that says *I'll deal with you later* and then turns back to Emily. "This is my date, Cory. Nate set us up." *What? There goes my swift exit.*

"Cory?" she asks, looking puzzled for a second before recovering. "Nice to see you again."

"Again?!" Nate blurts out in surprise before quickly schooling his features, looking at Shane for help.

"You've met before?" Shane asks, his eyes bouncing between the two of us.

"Yes," I say, looking at Shane but answering Nate. "We met in the bathroom earlier. Emily was..."

"I was trying to free my bracelets from my hair, and Cory kindly helped me."

"Of course, that would happen to you, Em. Luckily, this beautiful hero saved the day." Shane squeezes my hand and smiles. He's laying it on a little thick, but what can I do?

Nate's eyes flare at the same time Liv wraps her arms around him. An uncomfortable feeling takes over me at the sight of them, and I inwardly curse before biting my tongue to stop myself from verbally attacking her. This girl has her arms around my man, and I've yet to be introduced... That doesn't sit well with me. I need to get out of here. I need some breathing space before I give the game away.

"Who's getting me a drink?" I say to the group. I'm not usually that forward, but something tells me I'm going to need a lot of alcohol to get through tonight.

Chapter Thirteen

Cory

I'm significantly buzzed, Nate's borderline drunk, and it's only nine pm. We've barely said two words to each other all night between him playing pretend with Liv and me being coupled up with Shane.

If I didn't love Nate as much as I do, I would have left the second it got awkward, but I can't. After all, I'm part of the reason we're in this mess to begin with. Doesn't mean I'm fine with everything that's happening, though. In fact, it's quite the opposite.

"If you shoot any more daggers with your eyes, she's going to keel over," Shane says as he whirls me around the dance floor. "You have nothing to worry about. Whenever Emily's out of sight, it's easy to see that it's all an act."

I smile, even though he's wrong. Very wrong. Nate might be playing a part, but Liv? No, she's definitely not acting. If only my beautiful, naïve pain in the ass, Nate wasn't oblivious to it all. She's lucky I haven't walked over and slapped her for the crap she's pulling tonight. She may have the guys fooled, but, call it female intuition if you will, I'm telling you, she wants Nate back.

I look over to Nate, again, as Shane pulls me off the dance floor. I should be thankful that I can no longer see Liv's hands wrapped around Nate's neck, or her eyes staring up into his, but I'm not. I wish I knew how long I had to keep up this charade, because I'm almost at my limit.

Shane's been trying to help. He's been the doting date all night, much to Nate's annoyance. It's easy to see why he and Nate are friends. He's a great guy, he's fun and easygoing, and he can dance… He's a catch, but he's not Nate.

Lost in thought, I'm no longer paying attention to my surroundings, so it takes a moment to realize the room has gone quiet. Shane looks at me apologetically and cringes before steering me across the room. I open my mouth to speak but close it again when his soft smile morphs into a mischievous one.

I turn in time to see Nate's eyes widen and quickly bounce around the room. "Look after Cory for me while I jump up on stage for speeches," Shane says to Nate *and* Liv before walking away. It's obvious that while he's genuinely trying to help us in the situation, he's also enjoying making Nate jealous and uncomfortable. A little too much. I can't help but wonder if the show he's putting on is for someone else watching on.

I stand awkwardly next to Nate and Liv, trying to appear unaffected by this insane situation. Blinking a few times, I try to focus on the words, but nothing sinks in. I even wonder why Nate isn't doing a speech but can't bring myself to ask in case I somehow give us away.

I'm seconds away from taking another bathroom break, just to get away, when I hear Liv announce she's doing the same. As soon as she's gone, a warmth passes across my cheek, causing me to shiver. "I need to touch you," Nate whispers in my ear as we both continue looking toward the stage. He lightly brushes his hand against mine, causing me to inhale sharply.

My heart pounds in my chest as I try not to show a reaction, but the feel of him so close is twisting me up in knots. *Damn him and the effect he has on me.* I sigh and subtly lean my head back so I can whisper my reply. "You got us into this mess," I say, hoping he doesn't call me out on the fact that's not true. "There's nothing we can do about it now. It's only one more night, and—"

"Let's go home. Right now," he says, pulling on my hand. "Then the night's over. I don't care about Liv or my sister. I'm done."

Keeping my eyes on the stage, I shake my head, despite loving that idea. "We can't leave, Nate. You know that. Now, be quiet." Leaving together right now would draw the wrong attention. Especially with his sister standing a few feet away.

Nate does as I asked, even letting go of my hand, but he doesn't move away. The occasional touch of his skin lights me on fire, and I inwardly curse myself for suggesting all this. *One more night. That's if Liv's actually being honest and doesn't try to extend it. Eh! I shouldn't think like that. Maybe I have it all wrong.*

Liv returns and stands as close to Nate as physically possible. I want to stay calm, but I see red. Despite not being introduced, she knows who I am. She should be thanking me, not rubbing it in my face.

When the speeches are finally over, *thank God*, Shane joins us again and wraps his arms around my waist, smirking at Nate. This time, I'm not even mad about it, because Nate wasn't signaling for Liv to back off at all, either. *See how* that *feels, Nate.*

"Thanks for keeping my girl company," Shane says as his eyes flash to somewhere over my shoulder. "Now it's time to dance." *Oh, yeah, he's definitely doing this to send a message to someone else.* He's too involved for it to just be about teasing his best friend.

Nate tries hard to keep his cool, but I can see him fuming at Shane's hands around me. *Shit! This is about to get messy.* "Maybe we should—" I start, but Nate interrupts me.

"Do you mind if I dance with your woman? I'm sure Liv would love to catch up with you," he asks Shane with a fake smile. *Huh? I'm no object. Ask me!* Right now, I actually think I'd say no.

Shane laughs before turning to Liv. "Are you okay with that, Liv? Your man and my girl?" I cringe at his words and glare in his direction. "Too far?" he asks with an apologetic smile, turning to Nate without waiting for Liv's answer. "I'll give you one dance, Edwards, and then she's mine. Come on, Liv; let's catch up."

Nate wastes no time pulling me onto the packed dance floor as 'Ocean Drive' by Duke Dumont blasts through the speakers. I can't help but relate some lyrics to our situation. *How did we get here?*

We sway awkwardly to start, conscious of eyes that could be watching. But when more bodies join us, we're swallowed up by the crowd and no longer in view of anyone standing around. Nate grips my hips, pulling me closer, until there's no space between us. His hands run up and down my body, stopping dangerously close to the hemline of my skirt.

My breath catches when one of his hands makes its way up the back of my thigh, moving toward my ass. I spin around until my back rests against his chest, stopping him from getting where he wants. He groans in response, sending a shiver right through me.

"You can get through the rest of the night. After all, you have Liv if you need attention," I clip, but then cringe at my own words.

Nate growls at me, and when I look over his shoulder, his eyes are full of anger. "I can't wait, Cory. Fuck! You're irresistible, you're making my heart beat out of my chest, you smell delicious, and—"

"You're drunk," I finish for him.

He leans in to whisper in my ear, brushing his lips across my skin before he speaks. "Seeing him touch you, when I can't, is killing me. Don't make me do something I'll regret."

My head snaps back as I look at him in question. He smirks and pulls his lip into his mouth before continuing, "First, I'm going to kick his ass. Then I'm going to take you right here on the dance floor."

Shit! Sober Nate would never say that, but, God, it's so hot. *One more night, one more night.*

He raises an eyebrow just as Shane and Liv enter my line of sight, pulling me from my temporary haze.

"I've gotta use the bathroom. Be right back," I say as Shane reaches Nate's side. I dart away without waiting for a response, in desperate need of a cool down.

Splashing water on my face, I lean against the counter to control my breathing. The thought of someone, specifically Nate, being so desperate that he'd take me on the dance floor is a huge turn on, yet I'm so angry at him for the mess we're in. The mess I'm partly, okay mostly, to blame for. *But if I'd known that Liv wanted him back, I never would have... No, it's too late for hindsight.*

I exit the room ten minutes later, jumping when two strong arms grip my waist and push me to walk toward the back exit. I know it's Nate, not only by his smell, or the size of his hands, but by the way the touch of those hands sends an electric current straight to my heart.

I pull away and turn to face him, needing to get everything off my chest. "Are you ever planning on introducing me to your girlfriend, Nate?" I seethe before turning and walking away.

I don't get far before Nate's hand locks around my wrist, pulling me back to him. "She's *not* my girl," he grits out before moving us until we're facing the mirrored back door. "That," he says, running his hand up my chest until it reaches my jaw, holding my face in place towards my reflection. "*That* is my girl, right there."

As soon as the words are out of his mouth, he moves us out the exit and into the cold air.

The second the door closes shut behind us, Nate spins me around and crashes his lips to mine. My heart is beating so fast, and my mind is so full of lust, that I don't even hesitate. Instead, I jump up and wrap my legs around him. "Take me to the truck, Nate. Now!"

He groans out loud but obeys my command, carrying me to his truck. A truck that previously served no purpose, since neither of us is in any state to drive, but will now make the perfect privacy screen.

Nate pushes me against his door, out of sight of the building, and then grinds up into me. I cry out in pleasure before he silences me with a kiss, blindly opening the truck to push me inside.

I shuffle across until I hit the opposite side and then stare at Nate's large frame as he tries to figure out the best way to approach this. When he's reached a decision he slides in after me and sits in the passenger seat. He unbuckles his belt, unzips his jeans, and pulls them down before lifting to get a condom from his pocket. As soon as it's in place, he picks me up and positions me so I'm straddling his waist, hovering above him. The top of my head brushes the roof, almost uncomfortably, but I ignore it.

Nate moves my panties to the side, *thank God for dresses*, and pulls me down on top of him without warning, causing us both to cry out in pleasure and relief. The world stops as we stare into each other's eyes. Unmoving. After a month of no intimacy, this almost feels like too much. Our physical connection is so strong that I'm shaking involuntarily.

Nate pulls my face down until our foreheads are touching. "I've got you, Little Bit. I feel it, too."

He grips my hips and slowly moves me up and down until I'm able to find my own rhythm. It doesn't take long before we're rocking into each other with full force, breathlessly taking everything we need.

Nate thrusts up into me as I grind down on him, and the sounds of our bodies meeting is so loud that I should be self-conscious, but I'm not. Right now, I wouldn't even care if someone was peering through the window watching us. It feels too good to worry.

Nate snakes a hand up under my dress, pinching my nipple before pushing me back slightly so I'm resting against the dash. The new angle sends a spark right through me, and I scream out his name.

"Fuck, Cory. I need you to finish. I can't…"

I roll my hips forward on his next thrust, the movement, along with his words, sending me over the edge. I cry out in pleasure at the same time Nate finds his own release, and we ride out our high together.

As we come down, Nate wraps his arms around me and buries his head in my chest, hugging me tightly. "I've missed you so fucking much, Cory."

Gripping his face in my hands, I lift his head until his eyes are meeting mine. "I've missed you, too," I whisper, and press a kiss to his lips.

We stay like that for a few more minutes until we both re-member where we are. I laugh and hide my face in my hands as Nate chuckles along. "I never thought you'd be the sex-in-trucks type," he says with a laugh.

"I'm not, so don't get too attached to it." I climb off his lap, and he smirks, pulling up his pants as I move out of the truck.

"Wouldn't dream of it."

I adjust my clothes before we walk back inside, trying to maintain a straight face. Nate looks like he's just won a gold medal against his toughest rival, not hiding anything at all. I smack him in the chest and then squeeze his hand quickly, releasing it as we reach the door. "We should go in separately."

Nate glares at me as though I've wronged him, and I can't help the small laugh that escapes me. He links our hands and pulls me inside before coming to a halt.

My smile drops instantly as we come face to face with the two girls I very much wanted to avoid.

Chapter Fourteen
Nate

L iv and Emily are waiting inside the door, scowls in place and I internally groan. *Here we go.* I'm not in the mood.

"Nate, your sister—" Cory begins, trying to pull her hand from mine, but I no longer care.

"Fuck it. I'm done. Liv turns twenty-one in twenty-four hours. We're practically free."

"I don't think—"

"Do you think I'm stupid?" Emily yells, storming over like a child. I roll my eyes at her outburst.

"It depends. What about, specifically?" I snap, my big brother asshole switch flipping on with the heat of the moment. She rolls her eyes back at me and crosses her arms in front of herself.

"You just cheated on your girlfriend, with your best friend's girl, and clearly think that no one noticed... Or cares. How drunk are you?"

My eyes flick to Liv's to give her the chance to come clean, but she stares back in defiance. Okay, if she won't answer, I will. "Not that it's any of your business, but—"

"How could you, Nate?" Emily interrupts, and her eyes flash to Cory's. Cory's puzzled expression morphs into a smirk, and I make a note to ask her about it later as Emily continues. "I looked up to you. You're supposed to be a role model. But instead of staying loyal to your ex-girlfriend, who is clearly all wrong for you, you hook up with this wonderful human being standing beside me." Huh?

Liv's eyes shoot to Emily's in surprise as I furrow my brow in confusion. What the fuck did she just say? "I never wanted to be a role model for you. That's on you. How dare you say Cory's all wrong for me. You don't even know her. And Liv's not as wonderful as you might think." Cory snorts a laugh, but I ignore it. "You think you're angry with me? Well, I've got news, Em... I was never back with Liv. She had you all fooled. This girl right here is the love of my life. She was never dating Shane. He'd be lucky to get someone half as perfect."

"Nate—" Cory grips my arm to get my attention, but I ignore her again, determined to finish my rant.

"No, Cory, she—"

"Oh, would you stop? Please, stop." Emily says, sounding exasperated. "God, it's not me that's the stupid one. Nate, you told me about Cory. When you came home for spring break, you gushed about her before you'd even met. I put two and two together as soon as I heard her name. Plus, you've been staring at her like a lovesick puppy all night. So, if she's here, there's obviously something going on between you two. What I don't understand is the need for all your lies and shitty behavior." She turns to Liv, who hasn't said a word. "You, too. You both need to sort your shit out and stop playing games. For everyone's sake." And with that, she walks away.

"What the hell, Nate?" Liv yells as soon as she's gone. "You promised to help me. She'll probably run straight to your mom."

My eyes snap to hers as I reach for Cory's hand. "Actually, Cory made that promise, not me. Plus, it would have been fine if you hadn't shown up here and forced us to play house. Why are you here, anyway?"

"Because I wanted to talk, and I didn't think you'd bring her to a party with people from home, especially your sister." Her hands move to her hips as her anger increases. "I thought when you agreed to fake it with me that you were done with her." *What the actual fuck?* My eyes see red.

"I never said that. Why would I do that? I—" I start to defend myself but then stop. Tonight is on her. I need to go home.

Shane appears at that moment, and I thank my lucky stars. "Shane, we're crashing at your place tonight. Either come with us now or chuck me the keys."

Shane raises his eyebrows and smirks. "Please?"

"Please," I repeat, rolling my eyes before moving toward the exit. Shane and Cory in tow.

○ ○ ○

I hear the tell-tale signs of morning as my mind comes into focus. Birds are chirping, horns are blaring, someone's whispering in my ear. *Huh?*

I open my eyes and startle upright. My tired eyes lock on annoying cheerful ones, and I frown. *Why is Shane in my room? Shit! He's not. We're in his.* The previous night starts to come back to me, and I quickly check to make sure Cory is covered in a sheet.

"Why does my head hurt so much?" I ask an amused looking Shane, but I don't really need to hear the answer.

"You were pretty drunk for most of the night, but after fucking Cory in your truck..." I cringe at his words. "... Well, you upped the ante."

I rub my head as my brows furrow, trying to remember what went down after Cory and I *made love* in my truck. I was on such a happy high, what could have... *oh, right!*

"Yep, you made a huge scene about Cory being the love of your life and then demanded I take you both home. Once here, you got more shitfaced, and bitched about the fact that Liv was supposed to be your friend, but instead, forced you to endure blue balls for a month because your girlfriend is too caring." *Fuck, did I really say and do that?*

"Did I miss anything, Cory?" Shane asks, looking over my shoulder. I turn to see Cory smirking up at me, her head still on the pillow.

"Don't forget the 'my little sister's a brat' speech, though I'm pretty sure you were joking with that one." Cory adds, clearly enjoying the *let's pick on Nate* hour.

Groaning, I cover my face with my hands. "You two are no longer allowed to be friends."

Cory giggles, and the sound instantly relaxes me. I guess we're good again. Pity I can't remember exactly how that came to be.

Shane shakes his head as he pushes my shoulder, which in my hungover state has more impact than normal, sending me back down to the bed. He laughs and rolls his eyes. "Despite how fun this has been, I didn't come in to give you shit, Nate. I came to tell you I'm heading out."

"Oh, I was looking forward to getting to know you better. You know, without loud music and boyfriends giving me the evil eye," Cory says as she sits up. The sheet falls away to expose her fully clothed body, and I'm relieved to see that we didn't have sex again without me remembering it.

"Ah! I'm sorry..." Shane says, scratching his head. "Can we rain check?"

Cory smiles. "Of course we can. I just have one question." Shane raises his eyebrows as he waits for her to proceed. "Who were you trying to make jealous last night? I had assumed all the ladies were jumping at the chance to be with you. Who's resisting? Which one was she?"

"You mean he?" I add without thinking.

Cory and Shane both stare at me in shock. Cory because she's confused and Shane because he's... Well, he's confused, too, but for a different reason.

"You... You know?" he asks in a hoarse whisper.

I smile while shaking my head. "Of course, I know. I'm your best friend."

He continues to stare at me like he's unable to process my words, making me feel the need to clarify.

"You've been checking out guys for years. I've just been waiting for you to confide in me. At one point, I wasn't even sure *you knew*, but I've seen you subtly flirting with them, so that's not the case."

"Ahh... okay. Great. Great! It's not like I'm hiding it. I just haven't..."

"Whoa! I am not calling you out here. You are free to go at your own pace. I mentioned it by accident. I'm sorry."

I glance at Cory and find her gaze bouncing between Shane and I. A warm smile graces her lips. "Who was he?" she asks, jumping up onto her knees. "Tell me it was the tall blonde guy you were talking to at the bar. He was smoking hot. Or, omigosh, yes! Was it that guy with the tatts? Now, he's—"

"Easy there, Little Bit. Was it Shane trying to make these guys jealous, or are you trying to do it to me right now?"

Cory and Shane laugh before talking about the hot guy at the bar. Shane relaxes, making me wish I'd asked him about it sooner. He's always been a ladies' man, taking home different girls every time we went out, yet I often noticed his eyes lock on good looking men in his presence. Hopefully, no matter who it is, he finds someone worthy.

I tune back into the conversation just as Cory asks Shane if he's ever had a threesome. If I had water in my mouth, I would have spit it out all over the bed. *Who is this woman? And where is my innocent girlfriend?*

"Sorry, ladies and gentleman, question time is over," Shane says with a smile and a wink. "I really do have to go. Turns out, last night worked because the tatt guy asked me if I was free for lunch today."

"I knew it! Yes! Go, *go*! And call me with the details," Cory gushes.

I shake my head, knowing full well that Shane's not going to call her. He rolls his eyes playfully and walks out the door without giving Cory a response. I laugh at her cute little pout while squeezing her leg. "He's not really a kiss and tell guy, Little Bit. But we can call him tonight and press for details if you're that determined."

She smacks me with a pillow and squeals with laughter when I dive on top of her.

We make out until we're both breathless, making sure to stop before things turn serious. "God, was I that obnoxious last night?" I ask Cory with a sheepish grin.

"Yep," Cory says, popping the p. "Although you calmed down after I explained to you that Emily had actually called me wonderful, not Liv, and that you had it all wrong."

"Ugh! I should probably call Emily." I cringe at the memory of her walking away.

Cory nods. "And maybe Liv. She said she needed to talk," she adds, though she doesn't look overly thrilled about it.

"You're right. She's a friend, and I was pretty mean to her." *I was pretty shit to everyone last night.*

"But you weren't wrong. She didn't really think through her actions. And—"

"Ha! That's Liv for you. Let's forget about last night for a while. We have more important things to discuss," I say, wrapping my arms around Cory. I pull her into a hug, determined to salvage this day.

"Oh, yeah?" She smiles up at me but there's something off about it. "Like what?"

"Like what we're going to eat for breakfast?" I wink before smothering her in playful kisses, hoping we can work it all out.

○ ○ ○

When I get home in the early afternoon, I immediately crash on my bed, too exhausted to do anything else. Thank God the last few weeks are behind us. I never should have agreed to Cory's ridiculous plan. I should have tried harder to understand her reasons and worked through them with her, instead of letting her brush them off. She's going to be around for a long time. Forever, if I have my way. I need to make sure she feels secure in our relationship.

Huffing out a breath, I throw my arms over my face to get some shut eye, but the thought of Cory and forever has my thoughts running rampant.

My mind goes where it shouldn't. It's too soon. And yet, it can't hurt to be prepared, right? If you know, you know.

I shut down all negative thoughts as I grab my phone, calling my hero before I've even fully processed what I'm doing.

"Small bear. To what do I owe the pleasure? We only spoke a couple of days ago." I roll my eyes even though he can't see me. He's been calling me small bear forever, despite the fact that I'm now over six foot.

"Gramps, I've missed you. How's your shoulder going?" He tore his rotator cuff, doing things a man his age should never be doing. Being less active as a result has been hard on him. He's a tough nut, but I can see him struggling, so I try my best to call or visit often to cheer him up. In fact, I spend most of my college breaks at his place. Well, I did, until he got himself a *lady friend*... His words not mine.

"My shoulder still works; I consider myself lucky." That's Gramps to a tee, glass half full. "If you're calling about Christmas, tell your mom I'll be there. She doesn't have to use my favorite grandson to convince me." I laugh because I'm his only grandson, and that's definitely something my mom would do.

"I'm not calling for Mom. I'm calling for me."

"I'm listening." I hear shuffling, which means he's probably getting himself comfortable in his recliner, expecting me to vent. He's the one person, other than Shane, that I tell everything.

"I want to marry Cory," I blurt and am met with a chuckle on the other end of the line.

"Well, that's pretty obvious with the way you talk about her. Got any fresh news." *Smart ass.*

I take a deep breath and share why I really called. "I don't plan on asking her soon; things are still new. But I know she's it for me, and well... well, I was wondering if... if it would be okay—"

"She would have loved you to have her ring, Nate. And from what you've told me about Cory, I know she would have loved her, too. That's why you're calling, right?"

I clear my throat to stop the emotion threatening to rise. "Yes, that's why I'm calling. I'd love to one day propose with Gran's ring."

"I'll bring it to Christmas, or is that too late for your impatient mind?"

Shaking my head, I laugh again. "Christmas is perfect. Like I said, I don't have any immediate plans. It's just good to know I've got it if the moment presents itself."

I mean that. I don't want to propose tomorrow or even this week or this month. But I'm going to propose one day. If our time apart has taught me anything, it's that Cory is my number one priority, and I can't lose her. No matter what gets in our way.

"Does your mom know you feel this strongly?" *Including that...*

I groan, even though I should have expected that question. "Not *exactly*," I drawl. *God, I'm such a coward when it comes to Mom. She's so important to me, but ever since...*

"Nate, you need to toughen up. She's not the keeper of your life."

"I know that!" I'm not lying. I know I need to talk to her, but there's a reason I accepted a scholarship and moved away for college rather than using my parents' money near home. She's just impossible to tolerate on some things. My love life being one of them.

Gramps changes the subject, and we talk for a few more minutes. When I hang up, my smile remains in place. *Today is a good day.* Liv is twenty-one in a few hours, so she'll get her inheritance. Cory and I can finally get back on track, and after last night, we're in a good place. And, on top of all that, Gramps is letting me have Gran's ring to one day propose to my beautiful girl.

Yep, life is good.

Closing my eyes, I curl up to take advantage of the rare moment of silence I'm being awarded and drift off to sleep with thoughts of Cory running through my mind.

Chapter Fifteen

Nate

A week later, I'm cooking breakfast at the Ball House with Cory's arms wrapped around my waist. We've spent the last few days making up for lost time in every way possible.

Last night was our annual football fundraiser, so today's plan is to spend the day lazing around while recovering from yet another weekend of too much alcohol consumption. *So much for limiting alcohol during the season. Luckily, I have no plans to go pro.*

My phone rings as the toast pops, and I answer without looking at the screen. It's likely to be one of the boys wanting a ride home from wherever he ended up after the function.

"Yep," I say absentmindedly, shaking the whipped cream.

"Nathan, baby. Congratulations on your engagement. I'm so proud of you," Mom says, shocking the shit out of me and causing my phone and the canister to fly out of my hand, the latter hitting me in the nuts. "*Fuck!*" I whisper yell, biting my knuckle as I rub myself to soothe the pain. Cory shoots me a startled look as she picks my phone up off the counter.

A faint voice comes through the speaker. "Nathan? Are you there?" *Oh, right, I forgot there was something more painful for me to deal with than my aching balls.*

I take a deep breath, willing myself to stay calm. "What did you just say?" I ask through clenched teeth. I want to curse, but, since it's my mom, I keep my language clean. *Still, what the fuck?*

"I said congratulations on your engagement. Why else would I be calling on a Sunday during the day?" Yes, *silly me, why else would you be calling? Again, what the fuck?* "We're so pleased for you, honey. And you two were so sneaky. I didn't even know that you'd found time to meet up. But I'm so glad you did."

She's delusional, or drunk, or both. Maybe she's sick and hallucinating? I have to consider all these options, because if it's none of those things, then... *Oh shit!* Gramps wouldn't mention the ring, would he? No, he knows I wouldn't want him to. The only other alternative is that Liv fucked me over again, and I have no idea why.

"Who am I engaged to, Mom?" I ask, trying hard to not place blame until I have all the facts. Cory's eyes flash to mine as she drops into a seat. I inwardly curse myself for answering my phone.

We only just got things back on track. I won't let anything derail us now.

"Liv, dear. Who else would it be?"

"For fuck's sake! Are you kidding me with this?" *Oops, so much for not swearing.* Cory's eyes widen at my outburst, and she moves to leave the room, miming that she'll give me some privacy.

"No! Sit back down," I yell, scolding myself for transferring my anger to her. "Sorry, please stay." I smile, and she nods.

"Who's there?" Mom asks, not even acknowledging my swearing.

I sigh and calmly reply. "Mom, I think there's been a misunderstanding. I'm not engaged to Liv, or anyone, for that matter. I'm sorry for the confusion."

"Oh, nonsense. Of course, you are. I heard it from her directly." *God dammit, Liv. Well, that answers my question.* "I don't know why you're hiding it."

I close my eyes and take a deep breath because, again, she's my mom. *She's a good person, and I love her. Repeat, she's a good person.* We have a great relationship except where my love life or work life is concerned. She loves Liv like a daughter. A non-rebellious, always sweet, never distracting daughter, unlike my little devil of a sister. I get why she's pushing this, but I also know if she gave Cory half a chance she'd love her, too, maybe even more.

Liv and I were together for three and a half years, and before that, she was always around as a friend. It makes sense that Mom's attached to her, but this needs to end now.

"Mom, I'm *not* engaged to Liv. I will *never be* engaged to Liv. We're over. For good. I already told you this last week."

"Yes, but Liv—"

"I don't care what Liv said," I roar, barely stopping myself from throwing the phone. I'm lucky it didn't crack when I dropped it earlier.

"How can—"

"No, Mom. This discussion is over. I'll call Liv as soon as I hang up and sort this out. I'm sorry for the mix up."

I hang up without waiting for a reply. *What the actual* "fuck!" I yell, running my hands down my face as two warm arms embrace me from behind. "I'm sorry, Nate."

"You have nothing to be sorry about. She better have a damn good reason for lying again. She knows it's *you* I want to marry, *not* her. For *fuck's* sake. Why would she do that?"

I turn around to pull Cory into a proper hug and see a shocked expression on her face. She's staring up at me with wide eyes, and her bottom lip trapped between her teeth. *What did I say?*

She shakes her head, snapping herself out of her stare before cringing and taking a deep breath. "I'm pretty sure she's doing it because she wants you back."

I sigh because we've had this conversation before. "I know it may look that way, but I've known her my whole life, and while what she's doing is bullshit, she's not a liar or one to beat around the bush. If she wanted me back, she'd tell me. There must be another reason she's doing it now."

Cory shakes her head at me and shrugs. "Okay, Nate. But don't say I didn't warn you."

I wrap my arms around her, pulling her tight against me as I press my lips to her head. "I won't. Thank you. I'm sorry, Cory. I thought we were done with all this crap. But I'll sort it out. I promise."

I feel her nod against my chest as I kiss her head again. "God, I love you. I hope you know that."

Cory looks up at me with a small smile, and I'm thankful that she hasn't stormed out.

It's another week before I get Liv on the phone. I know she's dodging my calls. I'm diverted to voicemail a lot faster than I normally would be. If I hadn't had an away game last night and a planned lunch today, I would have flown home to track her ass down and set this thing straight.

Luckily for me, I don't have to do that. I'm heading out the door, on my way to Cory's, when my phone rings and her name finally flashes on the screen. "What the fuck, Liv?" I say, moving back inside and shutting the door.

"I'm sorry. I panicked."

"Why? You've got your inheritance. Why would you need to take the lie any further?"

"It has a thirty-day cooling-off period, something I didn't know about. You know, to make sure I'm not lying."

What? There are so many things wrong with that sentence. For one... "Liv. You *are* lying."

"I know that. But Gran and Pop can't find out. You're not the only one struggling with this, Nate. I have a boyfriend. He's not happy about it either."

"You have a boyfriend? Since when?" I ask a little suspiciously. She used to tell me everything. Not that it bothers me, but I feel like that piece of information might have helped things between Cory and me this past month. To know she was going through the same thing and to convince Cory that she wasn't trying to get me back.

"Not long, but long enough." *Okay, that's a vague answer. But not the issue right now.* I'm about to speak when she adds, "Please, just do this for me until they're happy."

"Ugh! Liv, I can't..." I growl and leave the words hanging in the air. *How the fuck is this my life?* While it sounds ridiculous, I'm not exactly up to date with family law, or *any* law, so I have to go with the innocent until proven guilty theory. Having said that, I really want to remind her grandparents that we are not living in the world of 'Days of our Lives', and they need to get their shit together and wake up to reality.

"Please, just hear me out."

I sigh. "Fine, I'll listen. Tell me what's going on. Every single detail."

By the time she's done, I feel sick to my stomach at the emotional abuse she's endured, but if I don't stop this now, it may never end. I know her grandparents. They're likely to take this lie and run with it so fast that I'll be married off before I know it.

"I'm sorry, Liv. I really am. But I can't help this time. It's going to ruin my relationship."

I'm met with dead silence at the end of the line. I think she probably expected me to agree to more lies. When she finally speaks, her voice is rough. "Can you give me a day?"

I run my hands down my face while reminding myself that this is Liv. She deserves a day. "Okay, Liv. I'll leave it to you. For. A. Day."

Hanging up the phone, I sigh, glad that the drama is finally over. Yes, it's over. Do you hear that, universe? Do not fuck with us again.

With that out of the way, I jump in my truck, tossing my phone onto the seat before pumping the tunes. I sing along to my favorite songs, feeling lighter than I have all week, so it's not until I pull up to her complex that I notice the time. Fuck! I'm so late.

I take the stairs two at a time and come to a stop when I see Summer, Dylan, and Joel hovering in the hallway. They look relieved to see me, so it's safe to assume Cory's freaking out.

"I'm here. Shit, I'm here," I yell as I run up the remaining steps.

"Thank God!" Dylan mumbles, but I ignore him.

I offer a quick 'family emergency' excuse as I run inside. Cory's the only one who needs a full explanation.

The second I'm through the door, I know I've fucked up. Cory's pacing the kitchen, cute brow furrowed in distress while mumbling to herself.

"Cory, I'm—"

She startles at my words and drops the bowl of salad she had in her hands. The contents spread out across the room and both of us stare down at the bowl as it rolls across the floor. As soon as it stops moving, Cory bursts into tears. Fuck!

I run to her side, wrapping my arms around her, but she pushes me away. "You're late because of her, aren't you?" She shoves me in the chest before covering her face with her hands. I stumble back, hitting the counter behind me and knocking something over.

Ignoring Cory's obvious desire to be away from me, I reach out and pull her into another hug, gripping her tightly. "I'm sorry. We need to talk about what has you so upset, but for now, it's sorted. I promise."

The front door opens at that moment, and the others file inside. It's only then that I notice water from an overturned pitcher spilling onto the floor.

* * *

No one asks us any questions throughout lunch, but I'm not naïve enough to believe they haven't figured out that something's going on. We try to act ourselves, but I can't be my usual happy self when I know Cory's hurting.

"So, Nate... Did you really win a karaoke championship as a kid?" Joel asks, causing Summer to choke on her drink.

All eyes flash to me, except for Dylan's. His are darting around the room in avoidance. This guy cannot keep his trap shut. First my Ferris Wheel phobia, and now this.

"I did," I say proudly, owning my achievements, even if they're embarrassing. "I sang 'Ain't No Sunshine'. It's my go-to."

"You're kidding me?" Cory asks, a look of complete surprise on her face.

"Should I be offended by that reaction?" I joke, causing everyone to laugh, including Cory.

"No, it's just. That song came on when we were in your truck once, and I had the strongest visual of you singing along."

Now, it's my turn to be surprised. I don't remember that happening. I always sing along when that song plays.

"I usually sing a different song every time I wind up at karaoke, but if I had to choose, my go-to song would be 'Do ya think I'm sexy' by Rod Stewart," Joel says, bouncing his eyebrows.

Summer whacks him in the chest. "It would not. I bet it would be something like... 'Kryptonite' by Three Doors Down."

"Ooh Three Doors Down, good one," Joel says. His eyes flash with something I can't read before he's back to his joking self. "I bet I'd even out-sing Nate with that number."

I scoff, and everyone laughs.

After we've all guessed each other's go-to songs, we clear up the table and the boys decide to call it a day. Cory and I wash the dishes in silence as Summer walks them out.

"I've got some studying to do," she announces when she walks back inside. "I'll see you kids later."

I don't miss the pointed look she gives me as she heads to her room. Cory doesn't look up from her cleaning task, but I can tell that she understands Summer is purposely leaving us alone.

I take the dish from Cory's hand, then pull her into another hug. *Don't worry, Summer. I'll fix this.* I have to.

Chapter Sixteen

Cory

The past few months have been an emotional roller-coaster, but Nate and I are finally in a good place now that we are free of Liv and her lies. In the aftermath of her announcing their engagement, I shut down. On the outside, things were great, but inside, I was slowly unraveling. I couldn't clear my head of Liv's hands all over Nate or the fact that she kept pulling him back in. She wants Nate. Of that, I'm sure. I know she claims to have a boyfriend, but why wasn't he ever mentioned before?

What worries me, on top of Liv wanting him back, is that despite everything he's told me, I still get this nagging feeling that a little part of him wants her, too. Like it's only a matter of time. Insecure and delusional? Maybe. But I can't help the way I feel. You can thank my last two boyfriends for that. Still, I'm trying to push that out of my mind, especially considering we're now on our way to Nate's parent's house for Christmas. That should definitely put my mind at ease. *Should* being the operative word.

I'm currently staring out the window of Nate's truck as he fiddles with the radio, but I'm not paying much attention to what's playing. I've been a ball of nerves since Nate invited me to his home, but I can't quite decide if it's because I'm finally meeting his parents or because of the way he asked me...

"Cory?" Summer waves a hand in front of my face when I'm lost in thought, which is a little embarrassing since we're surrounded by friends at the moment. "Hello? Where'd you go just now?"

"Huh?" I'd once again been thinking about the situation with Liv when I should be focussed on other things. Anything. That girl is taking up too much of my brain space lately, so my mind is definitely not at this party.

With it being Thanksgiving tomorrow, Dylan and his sister, Lucy, decided to throw a Friendsgiving party tonight. A lot of my favorite people are here, including Summer and Nate, Dylan and Joel, and Logan, who Summer and I have known since we were younger. I've even met a couple of new faces. Lucy, for one, who is lovely, and her boyfriend, who is not.

I've tried to keep my head in the celebrations, but sometimes, I just lose control of my thoughts and they drift, like now.

Summer smiles sympathetically when I don't answer her question. Ugh... What's that about? I'm obviously not doing a good job of hiding my issues.

"True or false, Nate talks dirty during sex." Logan asks with a mischievous grin. What?!

I stare at him in shock as most of the table erupts in laughter at my expense.

"Shut up, Logan," Summer says as she throws a fake pumpkin at him before turning to me. "That's not what you missed. Dylan was just asking about Christmas."

I smile thankfully at Summer and then look over at Dylan. "Sorry, Dylan, were you asking about our plans?"

"Actually, I was just saying that I'm guessing the big meet-the-parents is happening over Christmas. I bet you can't wait to introduce your girl, Nate."

I feel the heat rising up my chest as a nervous feeling takes over. Should I be concerned that he hasn't invited me home yet? I mean, *until now, I hadn't given it much thought because he hadn't been home. But with Dylan's assumption, and the realization that he's never even mentioned it as an idea, I'm now a little worried.*

Nate reaches over and links our hands, trying to get my attention. My eyes meet his as a hesitant smile forms on his face. "I was going to do this in private, but I actually wanted to ask you if you'd come home with me on the twentieth, for an early celebration, so we can be back here for Christmas Eve with your family."

My heart jumps a little as a nervous energy runs through me. He wants me to meet his parents. Unless he's just reacting to Dylan's question? No! Stop with the negative. The intelligent part of my brain is right; I need to stop worrying and start focusing on rebuilding our relationship.

Nate's brows furrow, and I realize I haven't answered. "Yes! I'd love to. I can't wait to meet your family. Please tell me your Gramps will be there."

"He sure will be." Nate smiles, lighting up his entire face with my question. "And he's excited to meet you."

My favorite Christmas song blasts through the speakers, making me jump as I'm pulled from my thoughts. I peer over at Nate to catch the end of a smirk as he tries to distract me from my nerves yet again. I glance down at the clock. Less than twenty minutes from his parents' house now, from the moment of truth. I swallow, again forcing myself to focus on other things... like Summer.

She's been a mess since our Friendsgiving, and while I'm definitely not the major cause of her pain, I *have* been in her bad books recently. Rightfully so, nevertheless, it broke me. Seeing her hurting and knowing I contributed to that was hard. Thankfully, she forgave me after a few days, and we're now back to normal. But, for a moment there... God, I don't even want to think about what it would be like without her in my life.

While I know I need to spend this time with Nate, leaving Summer behind on this trip has been hard, but my parents and Logan promised to check in on her. Logan had even threatened to kidnap her and take her on his boys' trip if he found her moping.

Nate clears his throat, and I realize I'm lost in thought again. "I swear, it's not about meeting your parents this time," I say with a laugh.

"Good, because they are going to love you."

I smile shyly in response, my insecurities rising to the surface again. *But what if they don't?* Nate's parents love Liv. Love her like a daughter. What if I fall short in replacing her? Or worse, what if they don't want me to replace her at all? *Stop it. That's not going to happen.*

Nate's hand curls around my thigh, giving me a squeeze. "I can feel the negativity pouring out of you. What can I do to distract you?" My eyes bounce to his with a devilish grin. *What can we do?*

"Not that," Nate says with a smirk, reading my dirty mind. "There's nowhere to pull over until we're practically there, and I'm not risking anyone seeing you in a compromising position. And the position I have in mind is very compromising." He winks as I shake my head with a smile.

"Okay, what can we do then?"

"Siiing. Off," Nate hollas, causing me to burst out laughing at the ridiculous tone of his voice. I don't hate the idea, though. We both love to sing... so why not?

"Done! I'll choose first." I clap with excitement.

Nate eyes me suspiciously before looking back at the road.

"'Shut up' Black Eyed Peas," I announce, grabbing Nate's phone to set it up as he groans beside me.

"Okay, but I'm singing Fergie's lines," he states plainly, with no room for negotiation.

"Deal." I smile. I love the hip hop lines, anyway.

We battle it out for a few songs until an idea comes to mind. I find the song I'm looking for and hit play, watching as Nate's eyes light up when the music begins.

"Is this a battle?" he asks, the smallest of smirks on his lips. Yeah, no. I'm not that stupid. I'm not going to battle against him with his go-to song.

"Nope, this one's all you." I smile as Nate's voice fills the car. *Holy shit!* If I wasn't already head over heels for this guy, listening to him sing 'Ain't No Sunshine' would definitely get me there.

We pull up at large electric gates just as the song is fading out. My eyes widen as I take in the house, no, the *manor*, the gates are trying to protect. *I'm so out of my league here.*

Nate grabs my hand as the metal structure opens, and I squeeze it, hoping to soak up some of his positive energy to replace my negative thoughts.

My already erratic heartbeat almost leaps out of my chest when we're greeted at the door by a man in a stiff suit. Closing my eyes, I take a deep breath and will myself to get through this. *I can do it. I can do it.*

◉ ◉ ◉

The house is quiet when we arrive, so Nate takes me straight up to his room to drop our bags. The second I'm inside, he pushes me against the closed door and crashes his lips to mine. I relax at the feel of his mouth molding with mine and open up to deepen the kiss before wrapping my arms around his neck.

"I'm doing this now because I need to feel you before we get stuck with my family for the next however many hours," Nate says, mumbling against my lips.

"I'm not complaining," I rasp, as he kisses his way down my neck. *God, I need this.*

"Dinner will be served in fifteen minutes," a voice booms from somewhere in the room.

My heart stills as I jump in fright, pushing Nate off me before straightening my dress. *What the hell?* My eyes scan the room for an intruder but come up empty.

A small chuckle sounds beside me, and I shoot a glare Nate's way. "It's an intercom, Little Bit," he says like it's no big deal. "No need to get your panties in a twist. Although that's something I could help you with." He reaches under my dress, but I slap his hand away.

"No way. I can't be sure that no one's watching us. Who has an intercom in their bedroom?"

"I do. And we will not be abstaining for the two days we're here. No chance. So, if it's not now, then get ready for me to make you so worked up during dinner that you're practically begging me to drag you into a bathroom to have my way with you."

I snort out a laugh but still choose option B. The moment has definitely passed for me right now. Plus, you heard the man. We only have fifteen minutes!

❁ ❁ ❁

When we enter the dining room, fourteen and a half minutes later, Nate freezes on the threshold, causing me to bump into him. "Geez, Nate, what–"

I stop right along with him when I see what caused it. Sitting next to Nate's sister, Emily, across from our two empty seats is Liv. She's deep in conversation with a woman I'm guessing is Nate's mother and hasn't even bothered to look up at our entrance. Emily, however, hasn't missed a thing. Her wide eyes lock on mine as she takes in what's sure to be a very awkward situation.

"Nate, Cory, welcome. Don't just stand there; come take a seat." A man who looks like an older version of Nate signals to the empty seats.

"Hi, Dad; it's good to see you," Nate says, finally making his way into the room.

He introduces me around, and it's only when we get to his mother that she stops talking and notices my presence. "Cory, it's so lovely of you to join us. Nate's told me nothing about you, so I look forward to getting to know everything." *What?*

I swallow a lump in my throat as my eyes shoot to Nate's. I feel sick. Nate shakes his head slightly as his grandfather interrupts my downward spiral. "Maybe you need to ask more questions, Sophie. I happen to know more about Cory than I know about Nate." He smiles warmly, and I melt before mouthing a quick thank you.

* * *

Turns out I wasn't wrong about the lunch being awkward. Nate's clearly pissed off with his mom but keeping tight-lipped. Emily is trying her best to include me in conversation, but getting railroaded by her mother into other conversations, and Liv has a smug look every time our eyes meet. *What the hell is that about?*

As soon as we've finished the main meal, I excuse myself to use one of the ten bathrooms for a much needed reprieve. I'm just about to head back when the door rattles. "Won't be a moment," I say politely, instead of what I really want to say... find another bathroom and eff off.

The rattling starts again, so I straighten my dress before stepping outside. Liv is leaning against the opposite wall. She's dressed to the nines in a tight, fitted dress, sky high stiletto heels, and heavy make-up. Compared to my winter dress and boots, she's a knockout. I smile politely, having nothing to say to her, and then walk away.

"Wait!" she calls, and I flinch before turning around. "I wanted to apologize for being here." *Okay, maybe I've read her all wrong.* "Sophie and Nathan insisted I attend, you know, as part of the family." *Maybe not.* I cringe but maintain a smile, refusing to let her get to me.

"I understand, and I appreciate the apology. Thank you. I better be getting back. Nate doesn't like to be away from me for too long." I wave as I turn away.

"Do you really think you're enough for him?" she says, the pleasant facade gone, her voice full of spite.

"I know I'm enough. But thank you for your concern." My own voice drips in honey by comparison. My plan being to kill her with kindness.

"Not buying it. You're too *nice* for him." She says nice like the word is poison, then continues in her pursuit to rattle me. "What are you going to do when he gets so angry he trashes the room? Or what about when he loses himself during sex and pounds into you with abandon? You know how rough he likes it." *What?* Her eyebrows raise in question as her lips curl into a vicious smirk.

My pulse spikes as I try to process her words. That's not Nate. She's lying. He doesn't... Memories come to mind of his trashed room when the mess with Liv first started, and the way I always felt like he was holding back something during sex. As if he was treating me like glass.

Liv laughs, and the sound reminds me of a villain. "Didn't know about either of those things, did you? Or maybe you're only now seeing the signs. Don't worry your pretty little face. He'd never hurt you, but you're too innocent and naïve to keep him interested long term."

With that, she storms into the bathroom and slams the door, leaving me frozen in place until I hear Nate calling my name.

I'm replaying her words as he reaches me and pulls me into a hug, kissing the top of my head. "God, I'm so sorry, Little Bit. I didn't know she'd be here, and I'm so fucking angry she is."

I hug him back but hold off replying in case I blurt out what I really want to say. *Are you really angry about it? You don't seem to be trashing the place... Stop it. She's lying. She has to be.*

We walk back to the room hand in hand, and the rest of the dinner goes by relatively smoothly. I spend the time talking to Nate's gramps and his partner and feel genuinely welcomed by them. The warmth they both show me does a lot to ease my concern, and by the time we retire to the living area, I'm feeling better about everything. I used the word *retire* because that's exactly what I was told we were doing. It's a whole different world here.

● ● ●

Emily and I are chatting about embarrassing Nate stories when he gets up to grab more drinks. I laugh, because I know he's really walking away from the current story I'm sharing, not wanting to be around when I reveal the punchline. Another fifteen minutes go by, and we're still on the same topic. *Turns out Nate's done a lot of embarrassing things.* When another five minutes pass, and he's still not back, my eyes scan the room involuntarily.

"He's taking his sweet ass time with those drinks. Let's go find him," Emily says with an understanding smile as she grabs my hand, pulling me to my feet.

"Sorry about Liv being here," she says, once we're out of earshot of the family. "She's lovely once you get to know her. I promise."

I smile because it's the right thing to do. Plus, she doesn't realize she's wrong. I'm sure Liv *is* lovely to her.

"Oh my God. I forgot to tell you about the time, Nate..." she trails off with a frown when we hear voices in the kitchen. Nate and Liv, to be specific.

"Even your mom wants us together, Nate. She knows Cory's not the one," Liv yells, causing Emily to gasp. The words aren't as shocking to me, considering what she told me earlier. She'll say anything to win Nate back.

I roll my eyes, about to interrupt, when Nate's mom calls from behind me. It's not loud enough for Nate and Liv to hear, but Emily and I turn.

She's standing with perfect posture and an unfazed expression. The look on her face alone has me cringing. "Liv's right, you know. Those two belong together. You're a lovely girl, and I wish you every bit of happiness, but it's not with my son. It's only a matter of time before he and Liv work things out, for good this time."

I stare at her, bewildered. *Was that real?* Tears form in my eyes as my breathing increases.

"What the Hell, Mom?" Emily hisses beside me. "Nate doesn't want Liv. He loves Cory. Liv doesn't want Nate, either. She's got a boyfriend."

"Nonsense. Of course she wants Nate. Why else would she be here trying to win him back? And watch your language, young lady."

"I really hope you're wrong, Mom. And you better have nothing to do with it," Emily seethes before turning to face me. "Come on, Cory. Let's see Nate, to set things straight. He needs to learn the truth."

She pushes open the kitchen door, and we both stop at the sight in front of us. A sight that makes me wish I'd stayed home.

Chapter Seventeen

Cory

Liv has her arms around Nate, and her lips pressed against his. His arms are down by his sides, unmoving, and he's obviously not kissing her back, but he's not pulling away either. Neither of them has noticed our presence, so we both instinctively stay still.

When Liv finally pulls away, she looks up into Nate's eyes with a gaze full of love. "I know you felt that, Nate. It was impossible not to."

"Shit!" Emily whispers beside me. It's quiet, but not quiet enough.

Nate's eyes flash to mine, widening on impact. "Cory, it's not what you think."

I know it's not, but I'm at breaking point. The pain displayed on Nate's face tipping me over the edge.

I run out of the room and down the hallway, trying to remember where the hell the bedrooms are. "Why the fuck does anyone need a house this big?" I say out loud as I turn around yet another wrong corner.

Nate catches up to me and grabs me from behind, lifting me into the air when I try to keep running. "Let me go, Nate."

"No! We need to talk about this. I didn't kiss her back. I didn't *want* to kiss her back. And I definitely didn't feel what she thought I did. I need you to know that."

"I know," I blurt with clenched teeth, still thrashing around in his arms.

"Then why are you running?" Nate grunts out, squeezing me a little tighter, so he doesn't lose his grip.

"It's too much, Nate. It's all too much. If you want to talk, put me down, and I'll talk, but I'm not sure you're going to like what I have to say."

He sighs and lowers my feet to the ground before turning me to face him. I take in our surroundings, wondering where we are in relation to the rest of the family. *Are they all listening in?*

Nate must think the same thing because he grabs my hands and pulls me into the closest room.

The heat hits me instantly as my eyes dance around the amazing sight before me. Blue shadows bounce off every surface, reflecting the water taking up eighty percent of the room. *Of course, they have an indoor pool.* Another thing to highlight the difference between mine and Nate's worlds. It's easy to forget when we're at college, but now...

Nate's staring at me with an anguished expression. Like always, he can read me and doesn't at all like what he sees. "I know what you're thinking, and you're wrong. I don't want this life, Cory. You *know* that."

"It's not the only issue, Nate. I told you Liv wanted you. I told you this would happen, and you didn't believe me."

He grabs his shoulder and sighs. "I know. I should have listened, but I thought you were projecting."

"What?!" I rear back like he hit me.

"I thought you were just letting your insecurities take over. I thought—"

"Wow! Thanks."

He winces. "Cory, that's not—"

"You don't even know what made me *insecure*," I say, even as I realize that's not entirely his fault.

Nate's eyebrows rise and then furrow. "That's because you change the subject *every time* I ask. How about you tell me now? Give me all the facts while we're sorting things out."

"I don't think that's what we're doing."

"Ugh! You're doing it again," he fumes, and the tone of his voice has me seething.

"The only two guys I've been with, other than you, treated me like dirt. Is that what you want to hear?" His shoulders drop, but he doesn't respond. "My first boyfriend was a virgin chaser. He said all the right things and showered me in compliments... Until we had sex. He left before I'd even had the chance to clean myself up. Boyfriend number two also treated me like royalty, yet I always felt like something was off. Turns out he was married to his high school sweetheart, and I was the other woman. *His secret.* I swore I'd never let a guy treat me like that again."

Nate looks murderous and sympathetic at the same time, if that's even possible. He pulls me into a hug and squeezes me tight. "I wish you'd told me, Cory. I would have done more to show you. I'll never do that to you."

"You have done it."

"What?" He pulls away, stunned, genuinely not seeing the pain he's caused by not being honest with me. "I'm nothing like them. Don't you dare put me in the same category. Our situation is nothing like the two you just described."

I wish that was true. I really do. But at the end of the day, I still wound up hurt. "I thought you were different," I whisper, unsure of what else to say.

"Did you?" Nate asks, moving in front of me until he has my attention. "Did you, Cory? Because right now, it feels like I never stood a chance. Like you were just waiting for me to fuck up." He's quiet, but his voice is coated in hurt and anger.

"You kissed her, Nate."

"She kissed me!" he yells, pointing to his chest. "I let her have her moment, hoping that she'd realize on her own that there's nothing between us. I don't want her."

"It's only a matter of time. Even your mom said so." His eyes flash to mine, but I don't let him say a word. "She's your ex, Nate. I can't compete with your history."

"Are you listening to yourself? She's my ex. E. X. I don't want to get back with her. She's my ex for a reason. Do you want to get back with the guys who hurt you?"

"No, of course not. But—"

"No but, Cory. You're being unreasonable." He shakes his head with a sigh. "I don't want to fight. What can we do to fix this?"

My heart cracks in two. Right now, I don't think we can fix this. There is far too much to process. The kiss. His mom's words. Liv's words. I don't even know where to begin.

"We fell hard and fast, Nate. I think maybe we need to take a breather. The stuff with your ex aside, you still lied to me."

"When? When did I lie?"

I sigh and sit on a concrete bench near the wall. "You said your parents would love me, but they were never going to accept me, and you knew it."

"I didn't know for sure. That's not... I didn't tell you because I wanted to protect you."

"You didn't even tell your mom about me. To me, that sounds like you knew. I just need some time."

Nate flinches at my words before gripping his shoulder. "How much time? Time never does anyone any favors."

"I don't know. I'm sorry."

He drops beside me with his face in his hands. "So what? You want the break you asked for when this drama all started?"

"No, Nate. It's not a break. It's a breakup. We're done."

"Like hell we are," he grunts, jumping to his feet with a look of devastation on his face. The expression quickly morphs into anger when he sees my blank stare. "This is not happening!" he yells, shoving a nearby statue that crashes to the ground. It breaks into pieces on impact, and I flinch as Liv's words flit back to my mind.

"I'm sorry, Nate."

"No, no! Cory, no."

"I love you, Nate, but it hurts to be with you, and I deserve better than that."

With those parting words, I run from the room, slamming the door just as something else crashes to the floor.

I find my way through the maze of hallways and make it out of the house before the first tear falls. I want to appear strong. I don't want any of them to see me crying. When I hit the pavement, I look around, no idea what I'm going to do or where I'm going to go. The door opens behind me, and I wince before walking a little faster.

"Cory, wait!" Emily yells, running out after me. I pause because she's been nothing but nice to me, yet I'm still on edge, nervous about what she's going to say. "Let me grab my car, and I'll take you wherever you need to go." I sag in relief and nod before following her.

"Where to, ma'am?" Emily asks in a cockney accident when I'm settled in my seat. She's trying to cheer me up, and while I appreciate it, smiling is a struggle right now.

"I don't even know," I answer honestly, dropping my head into my hands. "All my things are still inside your parents' place, and—"

"Do you need them? You've got your handbag, so you have the essentials. Is there anything else you need right away?" I look down at the bag over my shoulder. I don't even remember collecting it on my way out.

I rack my brain for anything that I might need in my suitcase and come up empty. It's just clothes and toiletries. Both of which I have more of at home. "Not really." I say, shaking my head.

Emily offers me a sympathetic smile. "Do you want me to take you to the airport?"

Do I? It seems extreme, but I've got nowhere else to go. "I think that's for the best," I say and then pull out my phone to text Summer, knowing it's about time I filled her in on my messy life.

Cory: I'm heading home. Can you pick me up from the airport in a few hours?

Emily's quiet for most of the trip, but as the signs for the airport get more frequent, she takes a deep breath, and I know a speech is coming.

"Nate's a dick. A gullible, blind, foolish, and sometimes intolerable dick." *Okay, not where I thought she would go with it.* "But..." *Here we go.* "I don't think he has any feelings for Liv." I cringe because she must have overheard our fight. "Did he miss the signs that she was trying to get him back? Yes. Did he make a mistake by not pulling away when she kissed him? Also, yes.

Fucking idiot." She mumbles the last bit under her breath and a small laugh escapes me.

"I still—"

"Oh, I know! You needed to dump his ass. Now that I see everything clearly, I know he needs to cut Liv out of his life, and the only way he's going to do that is to think he's losing you."

"That's not what I'm doing." I'm not trying to teach him a lesson. I'm guessing it seems like that, but I'm hurt by everything that happened... the lies, the kiss, the revelations.

When we pull up in a drop off bay, Emily turns to me and gently holds my arm. "I hope you and Nate can one day work things out because I'd love to have you in my life. Safe travels, Cory. I really hope I see you again soon." She smiles and shrugs, telling me she doesn't know what else to say, and I don't blame her.

"Thank you, Emily. For everything. You didn't have to stick up for me in front of your mom, and I really appreciate it. Even if Nate and I don't work out, you have my number. Call me anytime."

After another quick goodbye, I exit the car and head inside, ready to be done with this night. I've just reached the counter when my phone alerts me to a text. I don't check it until I'm through security and waiting for boarding. I have two messages.

Summer: Let me know your arrival time, and I'll be there to pick you up. I have ice cream and Sam Claflin ready to go. I love you. X

I can't help but laugh at her message. She knows exactly what I need to help with heartbreak, and I didn't even tell her what was wrong. I need sadness, other people's sadness, so I can cry my eyes out and pretend I'm crying for them. Sam's my man when it comes to those movies. Me Before You. Love, Rosie. The Hunger

Games. Okay, so the last one isn't the type of sadness you were expecting, but it's still a tear jerker in the end.

I take a deep breath and prepare myself for the second message waiting on my phone. Nate's. I know I should wait until I'm curled up on the couch, with Summer by my side, but curiosity will kill me, and now's as good a time as any.

Nate: You are my world, my sunshine. I'm so sorry I didn't do enough to make you believe that. I'm sorry that I didn't stand up for us. And I'm sorry that I didn't see through Liv's lies. But most of all, I'm sorry that I hurt you. I love you. Please don't let this be the end.

A drop of water lands on my screen, and I realize I'm crying. I wish more than anything that I could accept his apology and move on. That it was that simple. But it's not. And I honestly don't know what each new day will bring. Right now, I can't be with Nate. We need time apart. For how long? I don't know. Could be forever. Point is, I've got nothing more to give.

I meant what I said before I walked away. We're done. And I don't know if that meant for now or forever.

Chapter Eighteen

Nate

I'm sitting at the bar when I notice her walk in. *My sunshine.* God, I miss her. The last week's been hell. No matter how many times I replay what happened, I can't seem to figure out a way for it *not* to end like it did. Something tells me it was inevitable from the start.

When Emily returned home after dropping Cory off, I'd pulled her into my room and demanded she talk. I didn't get much out of her, except that Cory was flying home and Summer would be there to meet her. I took comfort in knowing she had her best friend.

Mom was the next to cop an earful. I let her get away with a lot, but in this case, I should have been more vocal. We nearly lost her when I was young. Someone randomly attacked her one night, and she wound up in hospital. It was a long time before she returned to being the woman before the attack. In fact, I'm not sure she ever did. Either way, I've tried hard to never get angry or upset with her, to never cause conflict, and I think that's affected me more than I realize. The things she said to Cory... Ugh! It makes me angry just thinking about it. There's no excuse for it.

My eyes flash back to Cory, because if anything can calm my thoughts, it's her. Seeing her here, at Riley's Bar, tonight, was the furthest thing from my mind. I assumed she'd be avoiding this place, avoiding *me*. Other than the Ball House, this is where the football team, me included, spend most of our time. Knowing she's here, that she came, even though I'd likely be here, gives me hope. Hope I have no business having.

I spend a good hour or more stealing glances her way, relishing in the fact that, occasionally, I catch her staring back. I don't even bother pretending I'm paying attention to the guys at my table. They're not stupid; they know where my interest lies. Not one of them has even tried to pull me into a conversation, and I'm grateful for it.

I've finally worked up the balls to approach Cory when Summer arrives. I flinch as my chest tightens. I haven't seen Summer around our group for a while. It's safe to assume she's here as backup. *Is it really that difficult to be around me?* Of course, it is. She probably would have left hours ago if it wasn't New Year's Eve.

I watch her for a bit longer until I can't take it anymore. I don't want to be around the loved-up couples or drunken hook-ups when midnight comes, so at eleven forty-five, I head out the back for some air. It's eerily quiet, considering it's such a big night. Most likely because everyone's indoors, wrapped up in excited anticipation for what's to come.

The door creaks behind me. Another poor soul needing to be alone on this night of celebration. I hear a sharp intake of breath, and I freeze, afraid that any sudden movement will send her running. *Cory.*

"Sorry, I didn't know you were out here," she blurts out in a rush. I turn my head just as she moves to walk back inside.

"Wait!" I cry out, raising my hand in the air as though I can physically stop her. "It's okay. There's plenty of space for us to both get air. You don't have to go back in."

She flinches a little but steps outside, moving toward the railing of the small patio.

We both stare out into the moonlight in silence. To the casual observer, we'd probably look like strangers. But if you could feel the tension, if you were standing between us, you'd know that's not the case. The air is practically zapping with electricity.

Cory sighs, breaking our quiet moment before turning to face me. "How have you been?" she asks, and those simple, every day words make my heart jump.

I angle my body to face her and mirror her stance. "Shitty," I say honestly. "You?"

"Same," she shrugs, like it's no big deal. Like I'm not standing here silently begging her to take me back, willing her to see how perfect we are, breaking at the thought of her never doing either of those things.

We fall silent again as the countdown begins inside.

Ten...

I take a step closer, then another, and another, until I'm standing right beside her. When she doesn't move away, I place my hand on the rail next to hers, making sure our pinkies briefly touch. Eyes focused on the world in front of her, she curls her finger through mine, sending an electric current shooting straight to my heart. I smile as we turn to face each other once more, but I'm met with a blank stare.

Five...

"I'm sorry," I rasp, brushing a lock of hair away from her face.

She takes in a sharp breath and looks down at the ground before whispering her response. "I'm sorry, too, for a lot of things. But..."

Three...

Nothing has changed. She doesn't need to say the words out loud for me to hear them and for my heart to crack.

"I'm sorry," I say again, mimicking her whisper, this time apologizing for what I've done, and for what I'm about to do. Her gaze lifts to mine, and I swear I still see the love and lust in the back of her eyes, through the look she's trying to hide behind.

One... Happy New Year!

I can't stop myself from crashing my lips into hers and pressing her back against the railing, my hands cupping her face.

Cory stills for a moment, so I do the same, my mouth locked on hers, waiting for her to pull away.

When she opens up and sucks on my tongue, I'm at her mercy. A deep, guttural groan rips from the back of my throat as she wraps her arms around my neck and pulls me into her, increasing the connection between us.

Our alone time doesn't last long as partygoers trickle outside. I push Cory deeper into the corner of the patio, releasing her face before grabbing her by the legs and lifting her into the air. She wraps herself around my body, just like she has a million times before, and moans when her core meets my hardness.

My hips move instinctively as I squeeze Cory's ass and try to pull her even closer. She grinds against me, matching my desperation with her own and then whispers in my ear. "We need privacy." *Fuck!*

Despite the now packed patio, no one's paying us attention as the fireworks and celebrations drown out everything else in the world. I rush us inside, to the first bathroom I can find, and lock the door behind us. When the light flicks on, I take in my surroundings and move towards the vanity, lowering Cory onto the counter.

The second her ass touches the cold surface; she pushes me away and jumps to her feet before spinning in my arms and leaning back against my chest. She rubs herself into my groin, working me until I'm at breaking point, and places her hands on the counter in front of her, arching her back to give me the most amazing view.

My hands move to the hem of her dress as I look up into the mirror. When my eyes catch hers in our reflection, her face flashes with a foreign expression. Something void of emotion. "I need you to be rough, Nate." *What?* My brows furrow in confusion. "I need you to forget who I am and lose control." *Again, what? That's not happening. Ever.*

Ignoring her words, I slide my fingers between her legs to distract her, but it doesn't work. She grabs my hand and raises it to her neck, squeezing us both until I'm sure it must hurt her.

"Cory, stop!" I yell, ripping my hand away as I step back, my eyes widening in shock. "What the hell are you doing? This isn't you."

"No, but it's you, right? That's how you like it?" *What the fuck?*

"Liv told me everything... How you prefer rough sex, how you trash things when you're angry," she seethes, moving away from me like I'm going to hurt her.

I take a step toward her and reach out a hand. "Cory, I'd never—"

She slaps my hand away, cutting me off. "I didn't believe her at first, given that I thought I knew everything about you. But then, by the pool, I *saw* it. You smashed that statue so easily, without even flinching. And just now, I could feel you holding back. Why would you keep those things secret, Nate?"

I stare at her in shock, taking in her words until she shakes her head and turns away.

"God, Cory. I don't know. It rarely happens when I'm with you. I just didn't think about it," I cry out, gripping my shoulder with a grimace. "I've only been that angry *twice* since we met, and *both* times were when I thought I was going to lose you. And I was right. I *lost* you. Of course, I was angry. But Cory, I'd never hurt you. I've never taken that anger out on another person. Ever." My voice breaks, and my chest tightens as tears prick my eyes. *How could she think that about me? After all we've been through.*

She's silent for a moment but then mumbles something I can't hear.

"Sorry, I didn't get that," I rasp, my voice full of emotion as it clogs my throat.

"What about the sex?" *Huh?* "Why don't you ever let yourself go with me?"

"Despite what Liv may have told you, I don't *only* like it rough. I'm not... I mean... *Fuck!*"

Running my hand through my hair, I growl in exasperation. *How the fuck do I explain this?*

My phone rings in my pocket, but I ignore it. Nothing is more important than this moment, right here.

"Cory, I don't want—"

Fuck! My phone rings again, cutting me off. I rip it from my jeans and silence it before throwing it on the counter.

"Cory, I've never even wanted to be rough with you. The way we... our... making love to you is far better than any rough sex I've ever had. The sex Liv's talking about is emotionless. When I lose all control and don't even care. I could never be that way with you because I love you too much." *There! Finally...*

She looks at me skeptically and opens her mouth to respond. From her expression, I'm not going to like what she says.

My phone lights up and vibrates on the laminate counter, drawing both our eyes. As soon as I see the name on the screen, I deflate. *Of course, this would happen.*

I expect Cory to get mad, maybe even storm out. What I don't expect is for her to answer the call, put it on speaker, and then shove it in my face. I'm too shocked to talk until Liv's voice whines in my ear.

"Are you ignoring me, babe?" I cringe at the term of endearment before clearing my throat. "I told you I was going to call you after midnight. Why'd it take so long for you to answer?" she continues.

I grunt by way of response; unsure of what else I can say.

"What's going on? Why aren't you talking? It doesn't sound very loud there. I thought you'd head out and celebrate."

Fuck! Why won't she take a hint that I'm not interested in talking to her? "Happy New Year, Liv. I've got to go." I need her off the phone, stat.

"Wait!" she calls, and for some stupid reason, I don't hang up. *Fuck my life.* "I wanted to let you know I'm looking forward to seeing you over spring break. It will be good to have you home for more than two days."

Fucking hell! How does she even know my plans?

This sounds so much worse than it is. Every word out of Liv's mouth is like another shovel full of dirt, clearing out my grave. Because make no mistake, she's burying me alive right now.

The second I hang up, midway through Liv's next sentence, Cory takes a step back and then sags to the ground.

She shakes her head before burying her face in her hands, sobbing. *Fuck!*

The sight of her shatters my already broken heart, and I fall to the floor in front of her. "What can I do? What do you need from me to stop those tears?"

She wipes under her eyes, looking up at me with so much hurt that I struggle to take in air. "Just give me space and leave me alone."

My heart stops. "What?"

"We're not together, Nate. We need to start acting like it."

"No, Cory. I thought... I mean... you kissed me back. I thought you just needed time. It's been a week." *This isn't happening. It can't be happening.*

"It's over, Nate."

I can't breathe. "For good? Or..."

"Just give me space," she says, standing to her feet.

That means there's still hope, right? I don't move from my position on the floor as she walks away, and as soon as she's out of eyesight, I crumble.

Chapter Nineteen

Nate

I 'm feeling damn good as I make my way through the yard. The sun is shining, the pool's full of beautiful, half-naked women, and I've got my boys. I'm also pretty *freaking* baked... For the first time ever.

"Baked. Baked. B... A... Ked. It's a funny word; don't you think?" I turn to see who's listening to me ramble, and when I find myself alone, I giggle uncontrollably. "Giggle. That's a funny word, too. Do men giggle?"

"Not usually," a voice says from behind me. "But I think we can give you a pass."

Dylan moves to my side and stares in the same direction I am. The only difference between the two of us is that he's focused on one particular girl, *his* girl, while I'm free to take my pick. *In theory.* In reality, I'm still hung up on a certain someone who just so happens to be walking in my peripheral vision. My heart clenches at the sight of her, and I inwardly curse. *Fuck! So much for feeling good. It's been months since I've seen her, and as much as I try, I can't move on. Probably because you don't want to. I scowl at my own thoughts.*

"She has some nerve showing up here after all this time," I say, keeping my eyes locked tight on the pool in front of me. A girl with bright red hair lifts herself out of the water with her eyes closed. Her bikini top is doing a terrible job of hiding what's beneath it, and her bottoms are almost non-existent. She's porn worthy, and yet, nothing. I feel nothing. "Do those brownies affect sexual desire?" *I thought they were supposed to stop the pain, not ruin me for other women.*

Dylan bursts out laughing beside me. "I'm seeing what you're seeing and don't feel an ounce of attraction. I'd say you're suffering from the same thing I am." *What the fuck?*

My eyes shoot to him in anger. "Did you give me some kind of disease? What the fuck do I have?"

Dylan's eyes widen in shock before he bursts out laughing again. "How many brownies have you had? I meant *love*, you jackass."

I scoff. "Who's in love? Not me. I'm done with that shit." I look back at the pool. *Maybe redheads just don't do it for me.*

"What were you saying before?" Dylan asks with a weirdly sly grin. *What's that about?* "Someone showed up?"

Oh, yeah, I forgot about my rant. I shake my head in annoyance. "I said that she shouldn't be here. This is my house. I live here. How dare she show up looking all hot in her short shorts and tight top, wearing that green color that brings out her eyes? I mean, what was she thinking?"

Dylan bites back a smirk, and my brows furrow in question. *Why isn't he as outraged as I am?*

"She's here for me," he says without a care. "You said I could invite whoever I wanted. You insisted on having the party here. What did you expect?"

"I expected her to stay away! I've done what she asked. I've given her space."

"And yet, you knew I'd invite her. I'd even say you wanted her here, in this place, to give you the home-ground advantage." He raises an eyebrow in challenge.

"Na-ah," I snap back. *That's definitely, most certainly, not what I did. I'm sure.*

"Na-ah?" he deadpans before shaking his head. "You are so gone."

"Whatever," I say, shrugging my shoulders because I'm cool. "I'm feeling good." His words mean nothing.

Dylan coughs out a laugh. "Fuck, Nate. No more brownies for you."

I roll my eyes but then laugh, too. He might be onto something, because while I am feeling very relaxed and lightheaded, I'm not at all like myself and maybe a little crazy.

"Want to swim?" I say, gesturing towards the pool. "Your woman is there, and I'm sure I could find one." I expect him to agree immediately, but his smile drops, replaced by a serious expression. I raise an eyebrow in question.

"Don't be a dick today, Nate." *Come again?* "You're both hurting. Don't do something you'll regret."

I frown in confusion as he walks away to meet his girl. As *if I would do something stupid.*

⚙ ⚙ ⚙

I did something stupid... really stupid. But oh so fucking good. I'm lying on the lounge by the pool, and I can't feel anything. I'm so relaxed that I don't think a hurricane would faze me right now.

I'm vaguely aware that I'm not alone, but I'm too far gone to care. Should I have resisted that last brownie? Probably. Did I? Fuck, no. Am I hungry? So freaking hungry.

A feeling of wet coolness moves from my ear to my chin, making me shiver all over. *That was weird.*

It happens a second time, and I can't decide if it's a good or bad feeling. I could open my eyes and check, but I'm just so comfortable, and—

Holy fuck!

I jump up from my seat and fall to the floor as a truckload of water soaks me to the core. *Well, that's sobering.*

My first instinct is to look up to the sky, to see what the hell happened, but instead of rain, I find Dylan and Joel glaring down at me. *What the fuck? I'm the one who got drenched.*

"Are you kidding me with this, Nate?" Dylan yells, pointing behind me.

I honestly have no idea what he's talking about. I was here, minding my business, when—

"Are you going to let them get away with soaking us, Nate?" *Us? Huh?*

My eyes move behind me to find a busty blonde perched on top of the chair I just vacated. My brows furrow in confusion. *Where did she come from?*

I shoot the guys an 'I got nothing' look and pull myself up. *Whoa! Easy there... maybe I should have moved to sit first.* Stabilizing myself, I catch Dylan's gaze to see his eyes narrow in disappointment.

"What? What!?" I yell, getting frustrated. And tired. *I think I need a nap. Ooh, yes, a nap would be great right about now. If only I could get past the... Focus, Nate.* "What did I do?" I ask.

"For one... you were pretty cozy with blondie over there," Dylan states, pointing at the girl beside me.

"Hey!" Blondie yells, but we all ignore her. In fact, I'd already forgotten she was there.

"And... number two?" I ask with a raised eyebrow.

Dylan practically roars at me. "You're acting like a fucking—"

"What Dylan's trying to say is that you're not acting like yourself, and it's hurting the people you love," Joel says with a steady voice, cutting Dylan off.

Dylan clears his throat. "What he said." *Huh? I still don't know what I did wrong, but I'm sure it's something I can apologize for tomorrow. Right now, I need food. What happened to the nap? Hmmm... nibbles in bed?*

I walk away without listening to another word.

●　●　●

I've just finished raiding the kitchen when I hear a loud bang at the back door. I peak around the corner in time to see an angel moving my way. She's beautiful with her long copper hair falling across one shoulder, her perfectly kissable lips covered in a glossy shine, and the most breathtaking eyes that are currently drilling a hole through my heart.

She moves closer, and I try to think of everything I want to say to her, but more specifically, what I want to say first.

Why couldn't you trust me?

I'm sorry.

You didn't even listen.

I miss you.

You broke my heart.

Can we just start over?

I hate you.

I love you.

She stops in front of me, and I open my mouth, prepared to unload all my feelings on her. But when our eyes lock, all of my thoughts disappear.

"Cory," I say with a nod.

"Nate," she replies.

Chapter Twenty

Cory

I hear Nate cursing in the kitchen when I step into the Ball House. I thought I was ready to talk to him, but now that we're alone, and after watching him outside, I don't know why I'm here. Actually, I know exactly why I'm here, but I'm not sure why I thought it was a good idea. *I need to leave.*

The back door slams shut, drawing Nate's attention, and I freeze. Emotion plays out all over his face, and I feel my heart start to crack. Taking a deep breath, I walk toward him, watching him closely as I mentally prepare myself for everything he's going to say. But when I'm standing in front of him, the only word that leaves his mouth is... "Cory."

I hold my emotions at bay, offering him a "Nate" in return, and when he opens his mouth to speak, I cut him off, wanting to be the first to talk. I need to know if this is all my fault.

"I know we have a lot to say to each other, but first, I'm sorry if I'm the one that caused the mess you're in."

Nate stares at me in confusion.

"If I caused you to... ah... take something."

His shoulders drop a little, but I can't tell why. "Nah, that's just my stupidity. You know... Embracing single life and all that." He shrugs.

Ouch! He's moved on. I knew it was a possibility, but I'd hoped ... My chest tightens as my pulse quickens. I somehow manage to keep my cool on the outside, maintaining my indifference, while inside, I'm hurting. "Yes, of course. Okay. Well, that's all I wanted to say, then." Total lie and he knows it. "I'm going to go."

I turn away before my facade cracks and walk toward the door, only making it halfway across the room when Nate calls out, and I break.

"Cory, wait! Please. Don't go." His voice wavers with emotion, but all I can do is stand frozen in place, in complete limbo.

"Please," Nate says again, making me jump when I realize he's suddenly right behind me, so close that he's almost touching me. His warm breath blows across my neck and my traitorous body shivers at the feel of it. "Please don't go. We need to talk." His voice breaks again and I give in.

I turn around, and my breath hitches at the sight of him up close. His bloodshot eyes mixed with disheveled hair and a pale face make him look ill. But it's the pleading look he's giving me, and the shallow breathing that really has me concerned. He's in no state to talk. Of that, I'm sure.

"Nate, I think anything that needs to be said should wait until you're sober."

He runs a hand down his face, shaking his head. When he looks back at me, his eyes are glassy. "I know. I know! But I'm so fucking scared that if you walk out that door, I'll never see you again."

My heart clenches and I swallow a lump in my throat. With everything that happened, I wanted to hate him. Hate him for the pain he caused, hate him for making me question our relationship, hate him for not fighting for us when I called it quits. But, as much as I tried, I couldn't hate him because I love him so much.

"Nate," I start, not really sure what I'm going to say. "I—"

"Stay, please. It's not that late, and the party's still going. Let me sleep it off."

Tears prick my eyes as I stare at the devastation in his. "Sleep it off? Nate, I need to go home so I can sleep. It's late for me. I'm emotionally burnt out. I can't..." I turn to walk away before the tears fall.

"Sleep here!" Nate calls desperately. "Take my bed, lock the door. I'll sleep on the couch. Please. Just don't walk out that door."

If I was made of glass, this would be the moment I shattered.

"Okay," I whisper before I've thought it through.

His eyes rise to mine in shock, causing my chest to tighten at the glimmer of hope I see there.

Without another word, Nate links our fingers and walks towards his room. He unlocks the door, holding it open for me to step inside before placing the key in my palm. The room is exactly as I remember it. In fact, nothing has changed. A photo of us is still displayed on his desk, and a pair of my shoes lay on the floor at the foot of his bed.

I can't do this. Why did I think I could do this? My throat constricts, and I clench my teeth, hoping to stop the flow of emotion. *Walk away, Nate. Please, walk away.*

"Well, I'll leave you to it," he says, and I almost sigh in relief.

"Thank you. I'll see you in the morning."

The second the door shuts, I drop onto the bed and burst into tears.

Chapter Twenty-One

Nate

H er cries are loud enough that I can hear them over the music pumping downstairs. Even in my hazy state, I could tell she was about to break, and she didn't want me there. I wanted to stay. Every fiber of my being struggled to walk away, knowing she was hurting, but I had to. If there was any chance we could fix this, it had to start with me letting her be.

I don't sleep on the couch like I said I would. It feels too far away from her. Instead, I curl up on the floor in Luke's room across the hall, praying that he doesn't bring anyone to his bed.

Despite being extremely uncomfortable, sleep comes easily, and before I know it, I'm being woken by the sun shining through the window. "Who the fuck left the curtain open?" I curse to myself.

"I did; it's my room." I look up to see Luke staring down at me. "Whatcha doing?" he asks, an amused look on his face.

I lift my head off the ground but immediately drop it back down. *Fuck, that hurts.* I deserve everything thrown my way, though. I should not have eaten those brownies. *What the fuck is wrong with me?*

Luke laughs as though he's reading my mind. "You were pretty fucked up yesterday. Did you think this was *your* room?"

I close my eyes before answering him. It would almost be better if I'd just stumbled in here by accident. "No, I'm here on purpose. Cory's in my room."

"Well, shit. What does that mean?"

"No idea." I say, but deep down I'm hoping it means something. It *has* to mean something, right?

"Then get off my floor and find out."

I grunt and roll over onto my back. "What time is it?"

"It's time to get the fuck out of my room."

"*Okay.*" Jeez. I try to lift my head a second time, and thankfully, it feels a little easier than the first. It takes a minute, but I finally manage to stand and make my way to the door. Luke starts a slow clap from behind me, and I flip him off as I leave.

The house is quiet, so it's safe to say it's still early. Hopefully, early enough that Cory hasn't snuck out. Pressing my ear to the door, I listen for movement but get nothing. I instructed her to lock up behind her and left her with the key, so I'm likely locked out, but I check the handle just in case.

When the door clicks open, my whole body deflates, knowing I'm going to find an empty room. Bracing myself, I push open the door and curse under my breath at what I find. Nothing, or more precisely, no *one*. The bed's perfectly made, the curtains are open, and her shoes are gone. *Fuck!*

I sit on the bed and drop my face into my hands. My one chance. I'm a fucking idiot. I knew she'd at the party. I fucking planned for it. Dylan was on the money when he said I'd offered to host it for him, hoping she'd show. But seeing her fucked with my head, and I made mistake after mistake. And now, I've lost her again.

I bite the inside of my cheek to stave off the emotion trying to break free. Clenching my fists, I press them into my eyes and groan. I can't cry. I don't deserve to be upset about this. It's my fault. God, I had—

"What's wrong? Has something happened?" A small panicked voice asks from above me. *She's here.* She didn't leave. I almost don't want to open my eyes in case I imagined it. "Nate, what's going on?" Cory asks again as her delicate fingers brush through my hair.

My beautiful, caring, too-sweet-for-her-own-good, Cory. She should be yelling at me. She should be outraged at my behavior, and yet, here she is, concerned for my well-being.

I look up into her beautiful glistening eyes and see all my emotions reflected back at me. She's hurting, just as much as I am, but she's here. She's trying.

"I thought you left," I rasp, wanting to be honest from the get go.

A soft smile plays on her lips, but it doesn't reach her eyes. "Do you really think I'd do that to you?"

"No, but I deserved it."

She sighs and then moves to sit on the desk chair in front of me. "You're right; you did. But I'm guessing you're feeling pretty sorry for yourself this morning, without me adding to it."

"Why are you being so nice? I heard you last night. I broke you; I broke us. Why aren't you yelling at me?"

"Because I meant it when I said we needed to talk, and I told you I'd stay so we could, no matter how hard it was." That's Cory, always one to keep her word.

I huff out a breath and then turn to look her in the eyes. "Where do I begin? I... Fuck, I miss you, Cory."

"I miss you, too," she whispers, then adds, "But that doesn't automatically fix things."

"I know," I say, leaning forward with my elbows on my knees, resting my face in my hands. "But I can't keep going like this. I'm sorry for not being honest with you. I'm sorry for not seeing what Liv was trying to do. You wanted time. I gave you time. How much more do you need?"

Cory sighs and shifts on the chair. She's nervous. "Is she still part of your life?" she asks after a beat. *Fuck!*

"In a way, yes." It's a shitty response, but the only one I can give.

"What does that even mean?" Cory asks, her voice breaking a little.

"It means that unfortunately she's *always* going to be in my life. But I haven't seen her since Christmas."

"Have you spoken to her?"

"Just that once. When you answered my phone."

She nods, but I can tell she's not convinced. "And..." *Told you.*

"And I don't know what else you want me to say. She calls. I don't answer. Moms finally backed off on getting us together, but she's not willing to cut Liv from her life. They have too much history."

Cory looks to the sky, like she's trying to find it in her to believe me. We've been here before. This is never going to work. She's never going to trust me again. The thought makes me mad.

"We were never going to work. Were we?" Cory's eyes drop to mine, and I can see regret there, but I don't wait for her to speak. I need to get this off my chest. "Despite the fact that Liv's around and wants me back, I *don't* want her back. I *never* wanted her back. But you never trusted me... No, you never trust *us* enough to see that." I pause for a minute as Cory continues to stare. "Why couldn't you see it? Why can't you see it now? There was never anyone else. It's always been *you*." My voice breaks just as the tears cascade down Cory's face.

We've both made mistakes, both been angry for stupid reasons. And even though it hurts me to think she doesn't see or trust how much I love her, I don't want to hurt her now. I never want to hurt her.

I reach across and pull her into my arms, engulfing her in a hug. Her whole body shakes with her tears, and I feel my own eyes water. I don't even know why she's crying, but I want to do anything I can to make it stop. "It's okay. You're okay. We can work through this. If you want to, we can fix this."

Her crying slows, and her breathing evens out as I rub my hand up and down her back. She takes a deep breath and then pulls back to look up into my eyes. "I broke us. It's all my fault," she says as the tears fall again.

"No," I state firmly as one of my own tears breaks free. Fuck! This isn't all on her. "Cory, we both messed up. We both—"

"But you're right," she says, sobbing now. "If I'd just trusted you... I've been seeing someone to help with my insecurities. I'm trying, Nate. I am, but sometimes I just... what if I'm not enough for you?" *What?*

All this time I thought she was angry with me, and she thought she wasn't enough...

I grab her face and lift it until she's looking me square in the eyes. "You have always been enough for me. Since the second I saw you on campus, you have been the *only* one that will *ever* be enough for me. You're more than enough. You're perfect. I've never been so sure of anything in my entire life."

Cory's eyes bounce between mine as more tears silently fall. "God, Nate. I—"

I take her lips in mine, not allowing her to finish her sentence. A sentence I'm almost positive was going to be an apology. One that's not needed. I'm ending this madness. Our forever begins again right now.

My lips gently caress hers, sucking and pulling as I go. Tasting the saltiness of her tears. When she moans, I pull away, needing to get everything sorted before we take this any further.

"I love you, Little Bit. I will always love you. I need you to be mine again. To tell me you're in this with me. That I'm not the only one who feels this way."

Cory smiles, taking a slight step back. She sniffles and wipes under her eyes before smirking. "How about you answer the question for me? If you're right, I'll take a step closer; if you're wrong, I'll move further away."

Fuck, yes! That's my answer right there. "You love me, too, Little Bit," I say confidently.

Cory jumps into my arms, and we crash down onto the bed. "Correct answer. You're the winner!"

Yes, I am. I laugh at her change in mood and then flip her onto her back before hovering above her.

"I guess it's time I took you on a first date," I say with the smallest of smirks.

Cory laughs, and my heart soars as I stare down at her breathtaking gaze. It's been a long time coming, but I finally have my beautiful girl back in my arms. Where she should be. Forever this time.

And just like that, my sunshine has returned.

Epilogue

Nate

I t feels like Déjà vu as we drive down the freeway towards my family home for Christmas. The roads are all the same, we're singing the same tunes, even the rental car looks similar to the one we got last year.

The differences, though, mean everything. Cory isn't nervous. At all. She's bouncing in her seat, chatting to me animatedly, while flitting through the songs on my phone. And, there is no chance in hell we are breaking up this time round. No siree; we are done with that shit.

When we arrive at the gates, Cory sits up straight and adjusts her clothes, staring ahead confidently. Here she is, my Little Bit of sunshine.

When we enter my bedroom, I'm no longer anxious about how the day will go. I don't need sex to distract me. Instead, I grab Cory's face in my hands and gently kiss her forehead. "I love you, Cory. Here's to a wonderful Christmas."

She smiles up at me with wide eyes and a warm smile, and like always, I lose myself in her. The Christmas party at my parents' last year was one of the worst days of my life. Even though we've been back at this house since then, having Cory here now means the world to me.

"What should we do to pass the time?" Cory asks just as the intercom comes to life with a request for dinner. *Thirty minutes.*

Cory jumps again. I don't think it's ever going to be something she gets used to, but she's adjusting to life with the Edwards family like a champ.

* * *

Lunch is uneventful this year, and fuck, am I happy about that. I meet Gramps in the games room as soon as the formalities of Christmas lunch are over, desperate to do this right away. The games room was always our space. Mom and Dad rarely ventured here unless they were looking for me. Gramps, on the other hand, would spend hours here with me, sprawled out on the couch, playing video games. Yep, he's a gamer.

"So, are you doing this thing today, or do I have to listen to you banging on about it for another year?" he says as soon as he enters the room.

I roll my eyes at the smirk he's giving me and laugh. "I'm doing it over the weekend. When we're back home. There's a party at the Ball House."

"What!? Why would you propose at the Ball House? You don't even live there. Kids these days... Nothing is private anymore. Hell, why not go all out and do it over the tube?"

I burst out laughing at his ridiculous response. "First, I'm proposing in the gardens. *Alone.* Second, you know it's called YouTube, Gramps. Your girl has her own channel."

"That she does. Just hit 10,000 subscribers last week." He beams proudly.

"Good for her," I say genuinely. Gramp's partner makes her own modest swimwear for ladies who actually want to show off some skin, despite their age; her words, not mine. She's actually doing pretty well for herself.

Gramps takes the ring from his pocket and places it on the couch between us. "Please take this off my hands. I've had it in my pocket since last Christmas," he says, taking a step back and raising his hands in the air.

"Shut it. You have not. Plus, you know why I didn't get it last year. Cory *had* just left me."

"True. Have I told you how much I like that girl?"

I blanch jokingly. "For leaving me?"

"Yep, you needed to see sense. But I also like her for taking you back."

"Me too, Gramps. Me too." I smile.

When Gramps and I walk back into the living room, Mom and Cory are deep in conversation. It was a long time coming, but after Cory left me, I finally stood up to my mom. We discussed my anger issues, the fact I avoid any confrontation with her, along with my plans to become a teacher and my feelings for Cory. Like Cory, I saw someone about my issues and quickly discovered it stemmed from my mom's attack and the feeling of being unable to control a situation when someone I loved was hurting. Mom came along to one of my sessions, and we talked things through. It's been great between us ever since.

Cory throws her head back and laughs as Mom covers her face with her hands, shaking her head with a smile. You'd swear these two have known each other their entire lives with how close they've become since we got back together. It didn't happen right away, but Mom worked hard to earn Cory's respect, and now... well, now it's hard to get them to shut up. We've attempted to visit more, and Mom and Dad have done the same. It's a relief to know that issue in our life is over.

Liv, on the other hand, is still around, but she's no longer causing trouble. She has a very different relationship with my family now, so even if she tried something, no one would allow it to happen.

"Nate, honey," Mom calls from her position on the floor. "Cory told me about your job change at work. I'm so happy you get to mix your two passions." She smiles at me lovingly, and I thank the heavens that she also accepted that part of my life. She's referring to my new role as a physical education teacher. It's what I always wanted to do, what I'm trained to do, and I'm lucky to have secured a role sooner than I thought.

"Thanks, Mom. I'm pretty excited."

"Lucky it's at the same school, too. Your apartment is in the perfect location for you both. You wouldn't want to give that up."

Our apartment. The apartment that Cory and I live in, together. I graduated not long after we got back together and secured a job a couple of months later. The boys said I could stay in the Ball House if I wanted, but I needed the change. And frankly, I wanted to be an adult. As soon as I made the decision in my head, I was on Cory's doorstep begging her to move in with me.

Was it crazy? Maybe. Were we moving too quickly? Probably. Did Cory say yes before the words were even out of my mouth? Abso-fucking-lutely.

After that, we found a great place, signed the lease, and moved in a few weeks later. The timing had even worked out for Summer, too, so if you ask me, it was all meant to be.

I smile at Mom when her amused stare brings me back to the present. "Yep, I'm a pretty lucky guy," I say in answer, although I'm not really talking about the job.

* * *

When the proposal day arrives, the Ball House is pumping like always. I haven't seen these guys for a while, so I do the rounds and catch up, all while keeping my hand very close to my pocket to protect the goods. After an hour, I'm done; I can't wait any longer. I'll have to make up for it another day. I signal to Summer across the yard, as she's helping me distract Cory, and then sneak away like planned.

It may not be original, but I've filled the space with tea candles and secured fairy lights to the tree and swing. Despite the sweat pouring down my back and my rapid heartbeat, I'm ready. Now, I just have to wait.

A few minutes later, I've moved to pacing territory when Cory's voice sounds behind me. "Nate?" she says in a quiet tone as her eyes roam around the garden. When they lock with mine, I see it. *She knows.* Her breath hitches, and she bites her lip before moving toward me slowly.

"What's going on?" she asks as I pull her into my arms.

"Nothing in particular. I just thought it would be nice to come back to the place where it all began." She stares at me for a second, and her eyes blink rapidly, as though she's trying to mesh what I'm saying with what she can see.

I move her toward the swing and then point to the lights when she's sitting down. "One of the guys set this up for a date with his girl. Nice, huh?" She smiles, but I see her deflate at my words, and it helps to remove every nervous thought from my body. She wants this, too. I shouldn't have lied, but I desperately want to surprise her.

Cory's silent after that, so I push her on the swing until she's moving at a nice pace. While she's still in full swing, I move to stand in front of her and laugh at her confused frown. Without my pushes, her momentum dies, and she slows down. *Perfect.*

"Cory, you once said we fell hard and fast, and you were right. I've never been so sure of something so quickly in all my life. I knew you were special from the moment I saw you. And after getting to know you, here, on this swing, I knew I was done for."

The swing slows even more as Cory stares at me, trying to hold back tears, completely aware of what I'm about to do.

"You are my world, my heart, my sunshine. I can't imagine my life without you."

I drop to my knee in front of her at the exact moment she comes to a complete stop.

"Cory Ann Walton. I love you. Will you do me the honor of becoming my wife?"

She gasps and jumps off the swing, falling into my arms. "Yes! One hundred percent, yes."

"Thank, fuck!" someone yells from somewhere in the garden as cheers ring out around us. *So much for being alone.*

Cory giggles and buries herself into my chest. I can picture her face flushing with embarrassment, but I also know that she won't mind. She loves these guys as much as I do.

Dylan's loud voice booms across the yard, causing Cory and me to laugh. "Come on, let's give these two lovebirds some space. Move along."

Like me, he's just visiting the Ball House for the Christmas celebrations, and everyone's thrilled he's back in town for a few days.

When the crowd has dispersed, Cory looks up from her position in my arms and smiles. "Did that really happen? It felt so real."

I laugh and pull her hand up to my lips. *Shit!* In all my nerves, I forget. Pulling the ring from my pocket, I hold Cory's finger and slide it on before kissing each of her knuckles. "There. Does it feel real now?"

Cory's hand flies to her mouth as she gasps again and tears fall. "Oh, Nate, it's beautiful... Wow... it's just... ah, it's perfect."

She throws her arms around me in excitement, and we fall to the ground. As soon as we've landed, Cory's lips meet mine, and that's where we stay, for how long I don't know, but just like Cory's ring... it's perfect.

We head home after our make-out session without saying good-bye. The second we're inside our apartment, before the door has even clicked shut, Cory's on me again. She leaps into my arms, wraps her legs around me, and slams her mouth to mine. I groan on impact because it's so fucking hot when she gets desperate like this.

"We're engaged," she says against my lips, barely pulling away to talk.

"We are," I grunt out at the same time she grinds down into me.

Cory kisses her way along my jaw and up my neck until she reaches my ear. "Have I told you how hot you look on your knees in front of me?"

I thrust up into her as I become uncomfortably hard, even though she's referring to the proposal. "Careful now. You're getting dangerously close to dirty talk," I say through gritted teeth, trying hard not to get too carried away just yet.

"I don't know what you're talking about, Nate." She giggles, and the sound is my undoing.

Dropping her feet to the ground, I unbutton her jeans and slide them down her legs. She's in the sexiest white lace thong I've ever seen, so I leave it in place, with thoughts of ripping it off later filling my mind. As soon as she's free of her pants, Cory takes control. Something she's been doing a lot lately, and I'm not complaining.

She pulls down my jeans and briefs before pushing me to sit on the couch. Straddling my legs, she lines herself up on top of me. "Hard and fast, Nate. Got it?"

I stare up into her eyes as both our chests rise as fall in sync. I've come to discover that losing all control doesn't have to mean it's emotionless. In fact, it can be quite the opposite. But while I love hard and fast, and sometimes even rough, I wasn't kidding when I said I preferred to make love to my girl.

But right now, that's not what Cory wants. And who am I to argue?

"Got it!" I grunt, rocking my hips up as she grinds down, burying me to the hilt. We both cry out in pleasure and pause for a second, adjusting to the depth, before all bets are off.

Cory digs her nails into my back as I bite down on her nipple and rock into her. When I roll my hips to change the angle, she grips my hair, almost ripping it from my head, and screams.

I thrust up into her as hard as she's pushing back, and when I feel that she's close, I pull her off my lap and flip her around until she's up on her fours. I rip her thong free from her body and pound into her again. She whimpers and drops to her elbows, burying her face in the couch. "Yes, Nate. Harder."

I slam into her over and over, working us both into a hot sweat as the sound of our bodies slapping together fills the air. When Cory tightens around me, I pull her up until her back is flush with my chest and wrap one hand around her neck as the other goes between her legs. She screams out in ecstasy, and I join her in her release. "Fuck, Cory, Fuck... Yes! Oh, God!" I cry out and shudder, in awe of the beautiful girl before me.

"Nope, it's just me," she whispers as we both collapse on the couch. I can't help the laugh that bursts out of me as I snuggle into her side.

Yep, I'm going to marry this girl as soon as possible. Maybe even tomorrow...

Thank you for reading Cory and Nate's story. If you want more from this loveable couple, they also appear in their friends future books in the Heartstrings series. Available now on Amazon and kindleunlimited.

WANT MORE FROM THE CHARACTERS IN AIN'T NO SUN-SHINE?

Ain't No Sunshine is a novella set in the Heartstrings universe and THE SERIES IS NOW COMPLETE. Dylan and Summer's story, When Nothing Else Matters, is available on Amazon, along with Joel and Delilah's story – Still Here Without You, Logan and Dani's story – It Had To Be Us, Lucy and Wes's story – Truly Madly Deeply Mine and Thomas and Lainey's story – A Sky Full of Stars.

The fun doesn't end there. Luke Bennett is getting a book as part of my new pro football series – San Francisco End Game. Beautiful Storm is available now for pre order.

Also by Katherine Jay

SAN FRANCISCO END GAME

Beautiful Storm (Luke and Amelia)

HEARTSTRINGS SERIES

When Nothing Else Matters (Dylan and Summer)
Still Here Without You (Joel and Delilah)
It Had To Be Us (Logan and Dani)
Truly Madly Deeply Mine (Wes and Lucy)
A Sky Full Of Stars (Thomas and Lainey)
Ain't No Sunshine Novella (Nate and Cory)

SYMPHONY OF SOUND DUET

The Sound Of Silence (Jesse and Willow)
The Sound Of Forever (Jesse and Willow)

AVAILABLE NOW ON AMAZON AND KINDLE UNLIMITED

For more information, visit
http://www.katherinejayauthor.com

And if you want to stay up to date with all things Katherine Jay, come and join my Facebook Reader Group – The Angsty Lovers Playlist — for fun, exclusive content and sneak peeks. Or sign up to my newsletter via my website.

Are you following me on social media? If not, you can find me on Instagram, Facebook and TikTok.

Acknowledgments

To be writing the acknowledgements right now feels very surreal. When I set out to finally complete one of the many ideas I had rolling around in my head, I never expected to release it. The idea for Ain't No Sunshine started while writing my debut novel, When Nothing Else Matters. It quickly became apparent that I had to write Cory and Nate's story and now, here we are. None of this could have happened without my super fabulous team, who I am forever grateful for.

To my writing pal, alpha reader and partner in crime Keelan, this book wouldn't exist without your constant help and support. I'm so thankful for everything you have done for me and can't wait for more plotting discussion, character chats, and Tucker... IYKUK.

To my amazing Beta Readers, Ree, Inka, Cass and Brittanee... Thank you! Thank you, thank you, thank you. Your feedback and ideas have been invaluable in bettering my stories, and I'm so grateful for your support and our chats.

A special thanks to my street team—you gals rock! I'm beyond humbled by the blind support you've shown me before even reading a word of my book. I hope this lived up to your expectations. I will forever be grateful for the friendships I've developed with each and every one of you.

Emily Wittig, your talent is undeniable. Thank you for your patience in designing my cover and for bringing my characters to life. I'm in love with the covers.

To my mum and mother-in-law, thank you for your unwavering support while I wrote this novella. Despite me never giving you any indication that I'll actually allow you to read my books, you've been there for me one hundred percent. If you are reading this... I'm sorry. Thanks to my Hubby and little ones. I know I've been busy, so I appreciate your patience and thank you for always being a big part of my cheer squad. Love you guys! And to my friends who have cheered me on from the sidelines... you know who you are... you are the best.

Finally, to my awesome readers, thank you so much for following me on this journey and taking a chance on a newbie author. I can't wait to share more stories with you in the future and am beyond grateful that you took the time to read this book. I love hearing your thoughts on my stories and characters, so feel free to reach out and share.

Interested in keeping up to date on all things Katherine Jay? Follow me on Instagram and TikTok, and sign up to my newsletter

to get first access to covers and blurbs, exclusive teasers and giveaways.

Thank you again for supporting indie authors. If you enjoyed this book, please shout it from the rooftops and leave a review on Amazon or Goodreads.

About Katherine Jay

Katherine lives in Australia with her three awesome boys-Hubby and two kiddies. She spends her days partaking in role play, building fortes and dancing. While her nights are spent reading and writing.

Her debut series, Heartstrings, is an emotional new adult romance with love that's worth fighting for and characters full of heart.